$\mathcal{A}$ CERTAIN TIME *of* LIFE

by
KATE BARNWELL

G

Also includes the short story

The Theatre on Latimer Street

and selected poems

After All

Last Evening

Temporary

What I Have Now

Other works by Kate Barnwell

Novels
'The Case of Aleister Stratton' by K.G.V. Barnwell
'A Worldly Tale Told of Mothy Chambers'

Poetry
A Collection of Poems & Lyrics
Every Truly Yours – 'Reflections on Love'

www.katebarnwell.com

A Certain Time of Life

ISBN 978-0-9935817-3-1

First published in 2020 by

Grosvenor Artist Management
32/32 Grosvenor Street
Mayfair
London
W1K 4QS

www.grosvenorartistmanagement.com

Copyright © Kate Barnwell

The moral right of the author has been asserted. All rights reserved. No part of this publication may be reproduced, stored in a retrieval system, or transmitted, in any form or by any means, without the prior permission in writing of the publisher, nor be otherwise circulated in any form of binding or cover other than that which it is published and without similar condition, including this condition being imposed on the subsequent purchaser.

A Certain Time of Life

Prologue	The Present 2018
Part I	Going to the Gallery, Year 1988
Part II	One week later, making plans
Part III	Arriving in Florence
Part IV	Walking tour
Part V	To the Cemetery
Part VI	A Day Out
Part VII	Two days on
Part VIII	End of day
Part IX	Talking to Arthur
Part X	Simon's story
Part XI	Leaving Florence
Part XII	The Heinegette Handkerchief
Part XIII	The Present, 2018 – Nina and Arthur's story, by Nina
Part XIV	The Present, 2018 – Nib returns home
Epilogue	Onwards and beyond

I look to myself, to whom
I was never really introduced
And see there, somewhere, smiles.
Hidden delight
Interspersed with reflections of woe

From the poem, After All

Prologue
The Present, 2018

Nib was 10 years old when his father died. At first, he mourned him quietly, then he was resentful. Yet over the years, as the heat of his anger lessened, he pieced together what he could until a whole new person was reborn to memory and, as Nib tried to shape his own life, he loved this distant man all over again.

Tall, broad, well-spoken and polite, Nib had qualities immediately distinguishing him from ordinary company. He had travelled the globe without communication and wandered its backstreets, seeking its secrets. Perhaps he was searching the roads his father had journeyed, trying to extract from these paths the same effects and emotions; in this way he might instil a little of the lost father into himself.

....

In a cosy cottage, the middle of five in a terraced row, in southern England, an envelope dropped to the mat. Nina picked it up and with a soft surprise noticed a postmark, eight days old, from Jordan and recognised the deliberate writing of her son. A pot of tea was brewing, she poured a mugful and added a drop of milk. She settled into her favourite armchair, pushing aside several books and a magazine. A curled tabby cat was sleeping on the opposite sofa; he stirred once to stretch his limbs and to check his clean paws and then snuggled his purring face into his furry chest. Nina read slowly and carefully the distant communication:

Dear Mum

I've arrived in a place I'm surprised to find very lonely... here I am at the entrance to the desert of Wadi Rum and the silence is deafening. A vast red plain of hot air; odd echoes carry on the wind, eroding the ancient rock. Now I'm somewhere so remote and isolated, in the midst of a geographical wonder, staring at an area so unusual and unfamiliar, it's made me think more clearly. This silence has given me a space... a void and I suppose I want to fill it with missing stories. I have searched and searched, but cannot know my father any better. I have resisted asking you, fearing it was too painful and perhaps it is... but it is only you who can tell me. So much time has passed, please write of him, his life and your life together... all those parts I cannot know, I need to know. I'm coming home, I miss you.

All my love,

Nib x

Nina took off her reading glasses, perched them in her hair and looked past the sofa into a middle-distance beyond the window pane. It was a rainy September morning and her eyes welled with tears. When she blinked them back loose teardrops fell onto Nib's letter just as his had done when trying to write and place these words. 'Yes, my love,' she said aloud, 'you're right, you should know about Arthur, of his life, his family and our love… I will tell you.'

The tabby cat yawned and mewed. He nudged the letter in her hand and drew a small smile.

Part I

Going to the Gallery, Year 1988

Mrs Hurst and her daughter, Nina, rapidly disembarked at Charing Cross train station and attempted to make a speedy exit.

Passing under the archway, adorned with advertisements, they saw an enormous poster of the Exhibition they were now bent on visiting at the National Gallery. Nina pointed, pleased to see it was two weeks until it ended. They separated briefly, dodging the solitary bodies of people, positioned like trees on a ski-course.

Mrs Hurst, with Nina behind (for in central London it was impossible to walk two abreast in rain or rush-hour) crossed two slippery intersections in conjunction with red lights holding back the stream of grey traffic. Keeping close to the over-hang of the city's edifices and with quick footing, they were able to skip little pools forming in the depressions of tarmac; care was required to avoid the dangerous, cracked and broken slabs of paving stone. While Mrs Hurst went to buy two, timed-entry tickets to the 'Colours and Contours' exhibition, Nina climbed the solid, worn steps to the gallery's portico in order to enjoy a wider panorama of Trafalgar Square. Catching the distant sound of Big Ben striking the hour, she turned to the chiming blue clock of St Martin-in-the-Fields and bowed her head to check her watch. She felt obliged and pleased to make the alteration, and set her life back two minutes in accordance with the bell-tower. In the time now earned, she scoured the townscape. In the already sodden square, people were darting about, preoccupied, caught in the unremitting rain. Swirling umbrellas and soaked-to-the-skin bodies flustered, scurrying frantically like startled and disturbed ants. The movement, the spinning and twisting of the umbrellas made the dullness dance; the sounds of honking cars, the pounding and stamping of feet and the nearby chattering and distant yells created a wild energy. As a painting, framed and hung in the gallery, this was the sound it captured in pigments. In two minutes here lay the smudged city landscape of Monet, the gliding, translucent, soft impression of Renoir. In troubled light and with artificial colour, art was made: translated, composed and beautified.

At the right fountain, looking outwards across the square, in amongst the kerfuffle, urban aggression and the vertical rain from which turmoil springs, someone was waving. A catchy, brisk wave; two arms blatantly beating the air and thrust directly towards the eight tall and smooth majestic columns of the portico under which Nina sheltered. It struck her eyeline immediately for he was the only human looking up and seemingly looking directly at *her*. He was tall, sporting a dark-brown fedora and a long, light-brown woollen coat with a red handkerchief flowing from the top left pocket, flapping up and down to his movements. Was the bright-red attention seeking, or indicative of danger? Who was he waving to? To her? She didn't know him. Turning left to right there was no apparent sign of reciprocation, no obvious recognition. Two girls were taking photographs, one man was fighting with a packet of sweets and two Spanish men were deciphering a plan of the gallery. No one was concerned or showed the slightest bit of interest. He carried on waving for what seemed an inexplicable length of time. It felt too long and Nina felt concerned. She was late for the exhibition and was now filled with a strangeness. She took out a tissue as if blowing her nose might clear her head. Here was a man in her vision who had broken the scene. He was not part of the turbulent crowd she had witnessed; his appearance had attracted her. He was looking out beyond the captured frame and signalling to the viewer. Was *she* the viewer? She was *a* viewer. What was he saying? Did she need someone to explain why the artist had placed him in the scene? But this wasn't art, this was real life. How peculiar. Again, she looked left to right, no-one saw him. So, she waved back, a fulsome friendly wave of acknowledgement. It seemed the most natural, honest and kind thing to do; people in the city were so often harsh and uncommunicative. Then, without a second thought, she turned quickly and hurried inside, moving to the deep comfort at the back of the warm gallery, to the scent of oil-paint, polish and coffee. Following the signs, she lifted her vision above the clusters of school-children, keen to catch sight of her mother.

"Have you seen the exhibition, *Colours and Contours?*" asked Mrs Hurst, "we're about to head in," indicating Nina as she came up behind Susie Levitt, a neighbour.

"No, no we're just leaving," Susie seemed very pleased, "just a coffee, then we're off. Hello Nina dear." Nina raised her head, conscious she still looked anxious about the waving man: thoughts of this oddity wandered over her mind.

Susie Levitt and her husband David, an Australian by birth, came to galleries in London for coffee and the gift shop. They did not see the paintings, the free displays or the paying exhibitions; they were not interested in real artwork and the pleasure in wandering from room to room, turning a corner to meet eye-to-eye the world's greatest works. They did not marvel at anything except a shop of colourful gifts and stationery. It was as if they didn't believe the gallery possessed the masterpieces indicated by the grand collection of postcards in the shops. Could they possibly believe the art on the mug or the notepad or the shawl or some such souvenir was devised for those pieces alone? Mrs Hurst didn't like to think these thoughts of Susie, of David, well he was Australian. Nina watched her mother form a familiar, stuck bottom lip. Mrs Hurst felt a little ashamed to think it was clearly David's country of origin that defined his ways and her logic. To the Levitts the gallery was one large tea-and-coffee institution, printing pleasant A6 picture-postcards to be sent in A5 envelopes to cousins on the other side of the world. Art was the reason for decorating a tin of mints or the design of a cravat.

"Just a coffee then we're off," Susie repeated to David.

She turned to Mrs Hurst, and Nina could read her mother's thoughts immediately, plain on her face.

"We've bought some Turner postcards for the kids and any portraits we could find." Susie held up a small paper sack.

"Might get one of those sunflower umbrellas as well," David grinned at Nina, whose hair was soggy and limp on her shoulders. "Looks like it's still raining." He had a sugary accent with a meter of constant sunniness and glee. Nina found him irritating and over-familiar. She smiled tightly, determined to remain unruffled by their ignorance. They were a funny couple presenting a humour you could not connect with and tendencies you could not blend with. Nina turned towards her mother.

"Let's go in now before something else happens," said Mrs Hurst, indicating the way through.

Nina owned such a warm, wide, uplifting face, always absorbing the world around her: observing it, living fully in it.

Mrs Hurst had had joy and wonders and she had had pain and upset but all this Nina would find for herself, no matter how much a mother tries to protect her child. So, she kept her tolerance, her esprit and elements of humour; age had made her more relaxed.

'Colours and Contours' was a selection of pastels on paper by the French Impressionist Edgar Degas. Most of the works had travelled from a public gallery in Glasgow, now closed for refurbishment, and hung alongside the National's own treasures. It was the first time some of the works had been displayed together and somehow, Nina thought, the collection complemented each other very well, without seeming too crowded or repetitive. The hand and eye of the artist was amongst them. The low light took a little adjusting to; some of the pieces were very small and fragile and many were worked on fine tracing paper. Nina knew instantly how much delight she would gain, peering and pondering from image to image, standing close beside the pieces, reading the snippets of information, then standing back to view them from a distance, framing the perspective and sensing the intimacy of the scenes. There were only three *salles*. Mrs Hurst liked to glide around the rooms first before focusing on her favourites while Nina took the methodical approach and went in order, following the guide set out by the curator.

She began with *vignettes:* men at a café, an expensively dressed woman in red holding binoculars, horses at the race-course. Then came examples of Degas' fascination with the ballet and behind the scenes ballerina poses. In some instances, the paper had been built up around the work to extend the picture from its moment of conception, when the artist was unsure how much his idea would grow or flow or how much to include; it was entirely fresh and unmodeled. The closeness was beautiful. The layers of colour, the long, thick strands of pastel, the movements or sense of chatter and distraction and private areas of concentration all fell from the picture into the quiet room. Nina felt a glow warm her, from the blood-red pastel tutus to the cosy crushed-velvet theatre box. The final room held private, keyhole moments: women bathing or combing their hair. Mrs Hurst and Nina viewed the pure white nakedness of a woman as she stepped carefully from her bath. Degas' touch was so tender. The contrast of the oval shapes and their soft contours: the lady's delicate behind and the smooth bathing tub. The colours, the white body and dark bath made a simple, emotive impression. This secluded, silent moment was a sight of warm allure and comeliness. Delivered in a mix of pastels, it made each woman sigh peacefully in a reciprocal softness equal to that of the artist's hand.

After the exhibition Mrs Hurst lingered on the edge of the shop weighing up the choices, as she did with every winter, of their day-return visit to London. Should they risk taking the later train and be back by dark and take tea in Bedford Street, or alternatively avoid the disparate groups of tourists making their way to Covent Garden, skip a served tea and opt for an early advantage with a takeaway cup and finish the crosswords at a window-seat table on the train? Certainly they could make it to the tearoom without getting too wet, but if it was still raining heavily, they may have to break with principle and buy one 'Monet-fashioned' umbrella.

Nina selected two postcards. She reached for a third card, 'Ballerinas rehearsing at the bar,' holding it up to the light she found the reproductions were nothing like the original. Suddenly Degas' use of red reminded her of the waving man in the square with the signal-red handkerchief, like a prick of consciousness.

"Thought I'd write a postcard for Aunt Merry and send it just before we get on the train… will just need to buy a stamp," Nina said, fanning herself with the card.

"Yes, she'll like a postcard from you. Might fill a gap in the wall of her windy house." Mrs Hurst smiled, "I wonder what she'll be up to this year."

explaining Aunt Merry

Aunt Merry, Mrs Hurst's older more exuberant sister, spent every new year planning to have one new, unusual adventure, which she then described at length on a separate sheet of paper tucked into a Christmas card of a robin. She had lived on the Romney Marshland of Kent for 30 years, marrying first one sickly vicar and then one elderly vicar. Her convent schooling would have been delighted at her devotion to church life and her commitment and continued support of spreading the word of God. Merry would have questioned God's desire to take from her so unkindly two very dear and dedicated men. It was His decision to do so, thus her life had been restructured and reformed into a new way of living: living every day with vigour and illumination, stimulation and enthusiasm.

Nina had visited her several times in the course of her own school-life when the holiday weeks gave time for long visits.

The Marshlands were flat and plain and very damp with an eerie, supernal wind that seemed to stir and twirl in confusing patterns as if the small area spun differently from its neighbours in the bordering county of East Sussex. Nina's vivid imagination, and the little she had read in Aunt Merry's Parish news, believed the winds to be the ghouls and spirits drawn by the points and lines of the land. On her journey to Kent she would look out for the fields with standing stones or the mounds of earth and grassy undulations hiding another era. Time and weather had played their part, disguising landscape and in part washing it away.

The remaining medieval churches of Romney Marsh now have a tiny but dedicated congregation with one vicar responsible for the rotating Sunday services and other Christian acts of celebration, dedication and service. Nina's favourite of the churches concurred with that of Aunt Merry's: St Thomas à Becket at Fairfield. The little church was built on a legend's tale. In the late 12th century the then Archbishop was wandering across the hazardous plain and fell into one of the many dykes, on his second fall, and in deep danger of drowning, he prayed to the newly canonised St Thomas à Becket and behold, a farmer, managing the land, saved him from a treacherous, watery grave. In gratitude for this miraculous intervention the church was dedicated to the saint.

Aunt Merry remembered the early winter times, travelling by boat to the little church. Years later she'd travelled to Venice where she'd ridden a gondola through the lagoon, dipping under the arched bridges or taken an imbalanced vaporetto with a flush of salty spray and maniacal captain, returning to the Lido, but nothing could match the small, English boat they had bravely sailed on Sundays to church. It was romantic because the little journey had held so much more. It had felt, and was, she supposed, like passing from one constantly disordered world into another calm and tranquil world, where *she* had found peace, and *others* salvation, and there was a constancy. Each week she helped to rescue and care for souls, finding the same healing and spiritual powers of the area others before had recognised. She delighted in the gift she'd been handed. By the time her second vicar husband had died, a chesty asthma and damp-spore allergy forced her to leave the isolated area and try the higher and dryer land and accommodation of Winchelsea. Here her modest rented cottage overlooked the fine church, right in the centre of the village, which she was extremely pleased to discover was named St Thomas the Martyr. Thus she felt that if she was to be bereaved twice in her life, it was St Thomas who would continue to look out for her and this time had guided her upwards: spiritually, she felt her soul was safe.

On learning her favourite poet of the moment, Dante Gabriel Rossetti, had visited and stayed in 1866, following in the footsteps of his friend, the painter John Everett Millais, she felt her artistic leanings fulfilled by proximity. Aunt Merry loved the sound of the artists' names, sometimes pronouncing them with alternate emphasis or with an accent or two.

And so it would be to another Thomas she would entrust her more adventurous self, travelling this time under the guidance of Thomas Cook.

Aunt Merry enjoyed the ballet. Three Christmas years in a row when she had use of her husband's family flat in central London, Meredith Smith had taken her very willing niece to the Coliseum to see The Nutcracker and to celebrate her birthday which fell on Christmas Eve. Meredith loved Christmas and every year she found her head swirling in all directions, particularly at the little supermarkets when people cried 'Merry Christmas!' She was sure, she would tell Nina, they were calling her name, Merry Smith. Then, as usual, on the Christmas occasion Nina did see Aunt Merry, the dear woman would recall the hilarity in class of her favourite school friend, Tish Chew. When the teachers called her name for register, for incomplete homework, for any school-related task, everyone would return the yells with 'bless you' pretending the teacher had sneezed. It became a common joke at school, and being a convent school, the teachers were quite happy to hear a chorus of 'bless you' hailed several times a day.

Aunt Merry was sprightly and charismatic. She had a lively intelligence and liked to do different things suddenly, without thinking them through too intensely. Her plans and ideas had, on the whole, always worked out. She brought out the better person in others, even those inclined to negativity or pessimism, and on occasion, Nina had enjoyed watching her aunt transform the grumpiest of men and the sourest of women to friendlier people as if it were a challenge; a test of her powers of positivity. She collected ticket stubs, postcards, theatre programmes and travel brochures, the latter two she had once lain entirely across her wooden floors in her draughty Winchelsea kitchen to keep out the cold, whistling winter winds. She was slipping on shiny, laminated booklets of Europe and the Caribbean islands for three months, sometimes replacing an old theatre programme for a more recent one and reading out-dated interviews and tailor-made excursions to destinations she had subsequently visited. Yes, it was time to contact Aunt Merry again two months into a chilly, but promising new year.

Nina and her mother

"Shall we go for tea now, in Bedford Street?" It was a rhetorical question, Mrs Hurst had made her choice. "I'd like to sit down, my knees ache and my back hurts and, by the look of the people coming in, the rain's stopped."

"Can I borrow five pence? Postcards are three for two," replied Nina.

"You can't borrow it, you can have it!" Mrs Hurst said kindly. "But let's go before I seize up."

Mrs Hurst's joints had a tendency to become sore in the cold. She liked to hold teapots or a hot water-bottle and rub a warming ointment into the twinge. She had forgotten the ointment and was annoyed.

The French tearoom on Bedford Street, Salon de thé d'Auguste, was Nina's favourite winter refuge in the whole of London. The glamorous interior made her feel like someone special and the delicacies were as much a work of art as a delicious treat. When she entered there was the scent of something sticky and sweet, the aroma of rose and pistachio or chocolate ganache. The sight of cream and custard layered between paper-thin pastry and chunks of sugared fruits sitting drunk and lazy in deep round tarts filled the eyes with colour and calmed the chilled soul. The tea was loose leaf, selected from the tea-chest, then hand-wrapped inside a muslin bag, served in individual teapots and poured into dainty cups with a slice of lemon in the summer or a dash of milk in the winter. Nina had a habit of lifting the lid to watch the steeping leaves swell and the tea strengthen: a strengthening she and her mother soon shared after two restorative pots. Nina nibbled a golden palmier, bits of the twisted heart-shaped flaky pastry crumbled onto her lap as she simultaneously attempted to write a postcard. And so, that afternoon in February, if you were to peruse the room of Salon de thé d'Auguste with its lavishly painted walls in the style of Boucher and its Rococo curled mirror-frames, you would find nothing unusual in partners, friends and family members sitting together, each in a style vastly removed from the world and era created around them.

With her daughter busy writing a postcard, Mrs Hurst was feeling slightly socially ignored. She had drained all the tea and had no handicraft or pastime of her own. She was glad therefore to spot a woman seated just beside her reading a book covered in tight plastic, a library-styled cellophane. After a few minutes (the woman was clearly waiting for someone) Mrs Hurst sparked a conversation about books, for a book was a belonging you could disturb.

"Is it good?" Mrs Hurst, leaned over and indicated, "the book?"

The woman looked down at the front cover as if she'd forgotten its title. "Yes, it's not bad, a sequel and better than the first."

She'd responded immediately and showed no signs of annoyance. Making a little pencil cross in the margin, marking her position in the novel, she then closed the book inserting a bookmark. She was about a third of the way through, Mrs Hurst observed. The woman was dressed in a warm fleecy jacket with a scarf on the back of her chair and a pair of folded gloves close to hand. The tables were so small in the café it was difficult to place anything safely without it falling to the ground and being dotted by crumbs or pastry flakes, some of which had floated directly from their own table.

"Is it from a library?" Mrs Hurst continued.

"Well yes, it is... our library's just reopened... saved by the council at the very last minute."

"Our library has just opened its doors too!" Mrs Hurst became animated. "A vast Victorian place, in need of a great deal of work and restoration... and modernisation, of course. There's a children's group, study area, something to suit everyone. It's full most days. I pop in for an audiobook or those large print books."

"It's a good sign, certainly." Her new-found friend countered, "we feared demolition or flat conversions."

They both nodded, comfortable in the equality of their concerns.

"Have you come far today?" Mrs Hurst moved the conversation on, she felt she might be boring about books. Her eyes had the remarkable ability to both scan and survey a room and to lock a person's attention as if you were the only one she had on her mind. She estimated Nina would be another few minutes.

"I've come from Glastonbury... and my friend," the woman said, pointing to an empty chair and a flimsy menu, "is London-based."

"The closer people are, the longer they take!" shrugged Mrs Hurst, sensing her library friend's slight disappointment at waiting and the natural glance to the cherub-coated clock.

"Well we're off, back to St Leonards!" she cried. Having seen the time Mrs Hurst relaxed a little. She had also come to a quick conclusion, she was feeling a little claustrophobic, hemmed in as she was by the festooned, swag-laden, putti-smooching, shell-decorated style of the Rococo. The lushness had become a little sickly.

"Oh! I have a friend who lives there… Fran Watson… no, she's divorced now… Fran Reed."

"That is funny… can't say I know the name." Mrs Hurst really didn't like it when people assumed you would know their friend out of a population of goodness 70,000 people? How often it happened to her. She tried not to look how she felt: bothered. 'You're doing your fed-up face' she thought to herself. She just couldn't mask her feelings but then the library woman couldn't read them so really there was no reason to worry.

"She's an artist, very talented." The woman persisted. She liked to nod her head regularly; she wanted to concur with everything. This was not a woman you would look to for interest or knowledge in furthering your political arguments.

Mrs Hurst bit her lip. Every other person in St Leonard's was an artist, a struggling one or a wondering one, talent was objective. Usually they were managing two jobs because very often creative art does not pay enough to fund a household or indeed the art itself.

The two ladies smiled and Mrs Hurst encouraged her new, seemingly abandoned friend back to her book. Pardoning the interruption, she turned back to Nina.

"Come on dear, let's go, are you finished? We can pay on the way out, the take-away counter is quieter. I've done it there before, they don't mind."

Mrs Hurst and Nina were sent back into the café area, where Mrs Hurst made a hushed fuss about queuing.

Their newly acquired warmth and recently enjoyed sustenance put a short shine onto the grey city. Stepping out into the bleak and failing light of February, the brightness of palette and paint from the exhibition and gilded decoration of the café had rendered only a temporary surge of energy to counteract the misery of the weather. The wetness now came in the form of rain-remnants. Rain that had fallen an hour earlier mixed with dirt, dripped from awnings and lampposts. Along the narrow street they dashed, avoiding the Covent Garden crawl of pedestrians and, once again, the broken concrete paving slabs that spurted water from the cracks and threatened your balance. Nina agreed to meet her mother at Charing Cross station while she popped into the nearby Post Office to send Aunt Merry's postcard.

The Post Office, a large, modern, impersonal building was, ironically, sandwiched between a greasy-spoon cafe and a slightly stale sandwich shop. Nearby leaned a grubby, paint-chipped corner pub. With its peeling façade and rather faded rustic charm it garnered a clutch of early-evening drinkers who formed a contrast to the post office's perfect efficiency. Opposite the pub on an angular corner was an old theatre, sister in soul and in life to the pub, only the better relation: smarter, cleaner and more aspirational.

Inside the Post Office, Nina caught her breath. She recognised the figure straight away: the waving man from Trafalgar Square. He was standing at one of the desks. With his hat in one hand he was searching for his wallet in the inner pocket of his coat; it *was* a light-brown, just as she'd observed. She'd paid more attention than she thought. She was at an advantage of course, entering the building minutes later than he, but still *she* didn't know him. No, not at all. Should she ask him: 'why were you waving at me?' But that sounded so odd. Maybe he hadn't been and she was muddled. It was hours ago, perhaps she'd imagined more than was there. She couldn't return to the scene like you could to a painting, and of course no-one talks to someone they don't know, especially in London. With the exception of her mother, who could strike up a conversation anytime. She hesitated, yet the confidence did not come and she continued waiting in frustrated inarticulation.

Nina was called forward to the booth next to the man; it was undeniably him. She asked the bespectacled clerk for a stamp and in response to a question from behind the glass she found herself whispering, 'yes, absolutely, without doubt.' This was really a confirmation of her feelings rather than a direct answer to her questioner. The waving man was dealing with a small parcel, apparently it was too plump to be a large letter and subsequently fell into another weight and size category. It was addressed in thick pen to a Signor in Florence. *'Firenze, Italia'* gleamed from the brown paper. He appeared slightly agitated and was insisting on an air mail sticker. All transactions were soon completed and the Post-Office was pleased to be finally closing, they were the last exchange of the day. The waving man turned. His face held the hue of one used to spending months in a warmer climate: a secure sun-bronze. It had taken years off his age. Nina guessed late forties. There was a general gentleness about his persona but it had been rustled, the eyes had been startled and he seemed a little edgy; it was impossible to hint at his personality. He did not ignore Nina, but he did not acknowledge her as a known friend, only just another person going about their business at exacting times. He positioned his hat stylishly on his head with an affable ease. Nina smiled, more to herself than to him, although he would have seen her smile. He turned back as if he'd forgotten something. Then, caught unaware, Nina sneezed. Overcome by embarrassment she felt confused in such a stale silence with the waving man only inches from her. With the kind of resolute calmness that's born of an internal confidence and without missing a beat, he handed her his handkerchief from the top-pocket, and said 'bless you.'

The handkerchief was bright, vivid red and delicately stitched around the rim; hand-painted flecks of yellow, pink and white, resembled the soft openness of rose-heads. As beautiful as beholding an icon, she handled it very carefully. It was body-warm and a little damp from the outdoors. The man moved suddenly, leaving the incident behind but remained just close enough to hear her faintly whisper, "thank-you!" So *her* path had crossed *the* path of this stranger; it was intimate and fleeting in equal measure. Then he was gone.

Checking her watch, Nina saw she must go too. It had all been so quick and strange. A new sort of strangeness, as if something had not ended but had just begun. A twist of fate, she supposed, but not something to dwell on. You don't dwell on wishes made on birthday cakes; it's better they find their own way into a truth.

Nina's imagination sat heavy, slowing her progress to Charing Cross. She boarded the packed train with her mother and with careful manoeuvring they were able to get seats. Nina faced backwards, while Mrs Hurst read the afternoon edition of the paper, facing forwards. Most passengers were weary from their working day. There was the sound of packets of crisps being crunched and fizzy drink-cans hissing and the coming and going of people as the train flowed and travel progressed. Doors opened and closed, steadily squeezing out exhausted home-seeking travellers.

As the first hour passed Nina began to touch on the scent of the country: damp woods and mossy trees. She thought of the waving man. She thought of the intimacy of his soft, silky handkerchief curled up in her pocket. She thought of the pastels and tutus and rich reds and pinks. Contrasting colours offsetting their beauty against pale paper backgrounds. Tender white flesh and sun-shined skin. Curls of pastry hearts and postcards. A parcel bound for Renaissance Florence. Aromatic, wet English fields. Her thoughts and images were rotating on a romantic loop: the waving man, the handkerchief. She drifted along, loving to dream and being excited by strangeness.

Part II

One week later, making plans

"I think you must go, no doubt whatsoever, you must you must… but how lovely, how kind, now that *is* an aunt! She wouldn't ask me, I know, but I'm twice as excited it should be you." Mrs Hurst was, to use her words, over-excited. She was also struggling to fathom a new, recently installed hob that required more concentration than she was prepared to give and as a consequence her coffee pot on maximum, was fizzing and spurting and tiny balls of hot coffee were spinning wildly and furiously, spitting onto the hot plate with hissing rage. New machinery was a nuisance and the principle of trial and error was still in production.

Twenty minutes earlier the phone had rung, the tone even sounded persistent. Nina had answered. What had ensued was a conversation that would change her life. It is not presumptuous to say it so plainly. Sometimes there are moments one can still recall clearly, for they were a turning point. For a while you had been on an ordinary road, a straight track and then up comes a round-about with new choices and new directions and you decide to follow a path from which a set of unusual adventures and occurrences come-about. Whoever believed in the straight and narrow was precisely made as those two words. Nina's present situation was slightly troubling and she was directionless. She worked as a part-time writer on the local 'Observer' newspaper, focusing mostly in the arts and culture section. She often found her stories tended to overlap into local history, local people and local enterprises. The problem was, it was all too local, not small enough to be small-town but not big enough to offer more expansive stories and ideas. In truth she felt her mind had more to offer and her soul demanded more of life. Sadly the paper and the local scene did not. They were ineffective in seeking out a better side to herself and thus she remained uninspired and increasingly disinterested, which was a terrible state to be in: neither did she wish to enter the hot-headed, shark-infested and back-stabbing world of a corporate city paper. Perhaps it was better to think yourself safe in the pond you were in, rather than suffering and drowning in much deeper, murkier waters.

Nina currently helped run her mother's small but progressive company. Mrs Hurst, Nina and her younger sister, who was working abroad, all benefited from a wise, early investment Mrs Hurst had made. Bringing a regular income from property and providing the family with a comfortable life had therefore reduced the pressure on her girls having to work all hours under stressful and aggressive conditions. This was something she had read so much about, particularly in the big cities and towns. This general ease of income did not lead to a complete and satisfied fulfilment of life. Life is very broad and Nina was truly bored.

"Nina it's me, Aunt Merry, I got your card – a lovely thing and I've had an idea. We'll talk about it tomorrow… not on the phone, phones are not for making plans. Can you meet me at Fortnums at half eleven, in The Parlour?" Aunt Merry did not like telephones. Her conversation, although not without character, was brief and to the point.

"Yes, I'm sure I can. Are you all right?" Since there was no worried or ill-sounding pitch to her aunt's voice, Nina thought firstly about her work, rather than any personal Aunt Merry panic. However sudden, it would be a good reason to finally give in her notice with a semi-honest and urgent excuse: 'family needs.' Another office-girl had left last month to fly to New Zealand with her boyfriend. She couldn't stop talking about it. She was determined to make a new start, she did have an adaptable personality. Nina didn't want to adapt she wanted to absorb: to be enlightened and entertained and elevated. She wanted to ask questions and find answers to some long unconsidered questions.

"Yes, yes I'm fine, it's just… I think we should take a trip together, maybe Rome or Milan or maybe Florence, yes. I don't know which! I'll have decided by tomorrow. I want you to come with me. Ma'll be ok. Listen, it came to me yesterday. Watching this rain, I can't stand it any longer. I'll pay of course…"

Nina wanted to say yes to things and to step out of the character people assumed of her; perhaps it was her own fault for exuding that kind of personality.

Somehow, being somewhere foreign and different with a little grasp of language but not total, it would be possible to find someone new inside herself.

"I can come, yes… Fortnums Parlour at 11.30… see you then," replied Nina.

"Marvellous, cheerio darling, see you tomorrow… love to Ma."

Aunt Merry hung up as quickly as she had dialled. It was as if the present really was blank paper ready to be filled with plans for the future. However ordered, spontaneous and peculiar her life, she did not always rush in to everything. She liked to rise early, rest in the afternoons and travel to slow down. And yet she had been known to rise late and live out the night in enormous style. 'Well if you're going to listen to jazz it has to be dark, very late and preferably smoky. I mean you can eat cereal in the evening but really, it's better as a breakfast dish. You know I'd listen to jazz all day but there's a time it's most suited to… indisputable.' Very often, trying to follow Aunt Merry's train of thought required a talent. How cereal and jazz could be sucked into the same sentence was typical of her. She had once connected God with nightclubs and the lifecycle of a bee with the Royal Opera House ballet performance. However, on reflection, she had made it all make sense.

Although Nina and Aunt Merry lived in the same county with a winding journey of roughly 40 minutes between them, London was the place where spirits were lifted and energy was both harnessed and zapped. Aunt Merry would come to town and 'put her face on.' She used to say this when they met together, and when Nina was younger she had visions of her aunt owning different faces, donning the most applicable one for the day. Then she realised it was simply a term for powdering her nose, adding a little lipstick and mascara and enhancing the light curls of her hair with comb and handy-hairspray. After a ten-minute use of these pencil-case items, she was ready to begin the day, whether it be the morning or evening. 'I'm ready darling!' she would say with a clap and a mischievous smile.

They had met at Fortnums' Parlour with a hug and were seated by 12pm to the chimes and percussion of the soldier clock outside the tall arched window.

This year Aunt Merry was seventy. "It's a different age, darling…" She clasped her hands together and rested them on the side of her face. "I've travelled, yes, but it's time for you to come along… I don't need caring for… just a bit of companionship and you're not doing anything… anything special… still typing and looking for a change?" Aunt Merry was forward, frank and often shockingly right, sometimes it hurt, but not if she could follow it with a solution.

"And how's Ma?" she continued, looking about the room. "This panelling's exquisite, look at the design up there… it's all hand-painted. See the foliage, very close work, very elaborate... See the use of foreshortening, from the figure's foot to leg, rising upwards to the cloud into a created space, all achieved by paint and hours of scrutiny. What talent and just for this room alone." Aunt Merry was pleased with her rhetoric, her inkling of smugness cast off by Nina who by instruction was twisting her head from side to side. "Got to use your eyes. I've learnt that on many-a-trip abroad. Crane your neck... but watch your step, that's the tourist's motto. Ha!"

There was no real need to reply to the first question. The answer held no heavy weight: her mother was very well. Aunt Merry had assumed so and was very pleased. Nina would not have come otherwise. And so her sister's good health and Nina's readiness to meet was a sure sign Merry's timing was perfect. A slight frostiness did exist between the two sisters, Merry and Celia, (Mrs Hurst). They were both generous, feisty, independent ladies and quarrelled occasionally as siblings do, only it had continued throughout adult life. Neither seemed able to converse without an edginess or irritability. Some sort of controversial tone, or insinuation of blame, reluctantly ignited the same hereditary fieriness. 'It's an un-put-out-able sort of thing,' one of Nina's Reverend uncles had said, 'no-one can sort it out, no-one but themselves, not even God.' This had been a surprise to Nina, 'I thought God could sort out everybody's problems,' she had said when very young and impressionable. It seemed, with a distinguishable huff and gasp from her uncle, who was slightly surprised to hear such conjecture from one so small, 'not even the Almighty can solve this one, except to send a rain to put out the fire.' Her uncle concluded the matter as if extracting and highlighting a message from the gospel; its absolute conviction undermined by a circumspect sermon. Nina was unconvinced and she thought her uncle was too.

They ordered tea for two with ice-cream and biscuits, and one double espresso. Seeing there were only two guests, the waitress queried the coffee on repeating the order. She was rather officious, Nina noted. Her aunt was oblivious to the manners and reactions of society to her ways and means. For many years she had broken with tradition and defied the norm, sometimes selecting a dessert before her main meal and insisting she work the menu backwards; waking either late or early between sleep patterns in accordance with the tide timetable, so she might swim safely at high tide before the currents turned; wearing an extravagant hat and a choicest title and taking herself to Eastbourne for the June tennis tournament with a delicious strawberry punnet in her handbag. She had been organised, sermonized and strict and restricted for much of her early life. Now she was approaching seventy, the thoughts and opinions of others did not matter, not like they did when one was young. Youth was not always fearless, it could be frightening.

Nina chose the pistachio gelato and mango sorbet, served in a coupe glass. Aunt Merry had blackcurrant sorbet and hazelnut gelato with a cornet hat on top which she used as a spoon to scoop the ice-cream and mop the chocolate sauce, (an extra cost of one pound) nibbling the edges of the wafer like a happy rabbit. It was difficult to talk and the contrast between the hot liquid and ice-cold cream set Aunt Merry's teeth 'on edge,' making her features contort into amusing faces, disrupting the face she had neatly assembled in the powder room half an hour earlier.

The persistent rain and monochrome wash of February had filled the month with shortened days of increased gloom. The hours had been repetitive, rolling from dull morning to dark evening as if each of the brief days were being knitted into a shroud that could only be cast off by the arrival of March winds. The recent exhibition at the National Gallery had brought a welcome flood of colour and of course the handkerchief, which Nina kept tucked in her pocket, not to use, but to feel; one feel conjured many feelings.

Out of the tall, glass-paned, polished window, remarkably untouched by dirty rain, Fortnums was impeccably clean. Inside and outside, a haven, always at the ready for a potential impromptu Royal visit. Nina watched the dense clouds begin to lift, push apart and allow a daytime blue to sigh across the sky. A wide, welcome ray of sun fell upon the long stone building of the Royal Academy opposite. The classic columns were visibly soaking up a new warmth. Nina knew that, through the archway entrance, the statues of the great Royal Academicians, high in their niches, could relax their solid limbs. Nina and Merry remained in shadow but the borrowed light and reflection offered them both a transitory moment of optimism. So clearly, under this depressing winter cloud lay the potential for a breadth and energy, and as the wind finally broke the bulk, the sun delivered its promised hope. Aunt Merry had seen the change in the weather's fortune and felt the richer for it. Her idea to escape abroad for a few weeks had been approved. She had received a good sign.

"Ah!" cried Aunt Merry, "it's the westerly wind god, Zephyr… Z E P H Y R." She always exalted in finding a reason to drop a learned name into everyday life, a characteristic she had kept from her church days. A god or goddess was often the source of a moment's joy and sometimes displeasure. She liked to think the gods provided rational motives to the circumstances of her choosing. Today it was clearly Zephyr who had designed the split and tricks of the sky.

"He's come to chase the clouds away with his light spring and early summer breezes!" Just as the clouds lifted so would her mood and attitude. She watched a couple order another selection of biscuits and a little boy cry for a second ice-cream, his mother smiling sweetly, naturally succumbed. Two young ladies opted to sit at a corner-booth table designed for four, instead of the parlour bar, and not one smartly dressed waiter batted an eyelid.

'Hmm', she had nodded in satisfaction, 'Zephyr sends away the gloom and the rooms are filled with happier people, generous to themselves and others.'

The sun, having been concealed for so long by grey obscurity, finally stretched its beams over Earth like a goodly giant extending a hand to a child. From the shafts of righteous light came a warm pleasantness and cheer. The only exception seemed to be a sour waitress, whose face had been frozen glum by the long winter; it would take much more to melt her. Perhaps, thought Aunt Merry, it was her heart that needed attention, in which case it would take more than a sunbeam to raise some sparkle to her cheeks.

"But it's only February... Spring and Summer, they're ages away," said Nina.

"We are the better side of the year, at least!" said Aunt Merry. She would not be dispirited. "It is February all over the world, I suggest we find someone else's April." Aunt Merry looked keenly at Nina.

"Yes, that'll give you time to make arrangements... three weeks should be a good length of time away. We'll both undergo a sort of... Renaissance... one's changing and evolving all the time... but I sense you are stuck Nina... stuck and a bit unhappy?"

Nina felt affronted. She blushed because it was true, her objections retaliated. She was not only tired of dismal winters, of monotony and predictable routines, she was tired of herself and this was inescapable. Three days previously she'd looked in the mirror and wondered what could she do to make herself attractive, to shine with confidence. Inside she felt vacant and lost. She considered herself part of a camouflaged crowd, linked by pattern and ordinariness. Day by day and week by week following peak-hour people as structured as herself, each to his or her work destination, building up a small sum of money to take themselves away on a summery trip, then returning home to continue the same cycle. The recharged energy seeped out far faster than the time taken to revive it. A harsh and honest reality faced her. Quickly she realised it would have to be something or someone who'd help her find the inner beauty she longed to possess. She felt prettier just by holding the handkerchief and running her fingers over the stitching and her thumb over the painted flowers; they were slightly raised and, after only a day, she was certain she could tell the difference between the splashes of colour. It was a good test, if oddly childish and in some way it made her happy. Happiness can be found in oddness as in strangeness too.

Aunt Merry would counsel, she had a direct yet persuasive approach. She would discuss guardian angels as naturally as discussing hairdressers and remark, "the Fates of classical mythology, Fates with a capital 'F' mind you, were three goddesses of destiny, and being women, they would listen, determine the course of your life… you just have to be bright enough to see the signs they send and then steer your own direction."

In the Parlour a gentle hum of socialness, no one voice louder than another, and the chink of cups and saucers continued uninterrupted from morning coffee to afternoon tea. Nowadays Fortnums collected a miscellaneous crowd of people and looking about the tables Nina wondered what had gathered them there that particular day. It was the day her aunt would announce her news, "I've decided it's to be Florence, three weeks in Florence! If we, well certainly *you*, are to have a re-birth then there is no better place than the Renaissance city." She clapped her hands with enthusiasm. "I did it so briefly when I went two or three years ago… Gosh they all roll into one… what does it matter? We, or you, or both of us, can do as much or as little as we want, but we shall have the time and you can… can set your own pace." Aunt Merry was forming her plan. She was painting with words, a whole picture of colour, excitement and knowledge to fill her canvas.

"Tommy knows a wonderful hotel, an old merchant house, beside the river, with a terrace view over all of the city. He sent me a postcard… see how postcards still work!" She winked, giving a little credit to Nina's thoughtful correspondence. Nina was beginning to fade, the colour from her cheeks began to drain, the heat lifted from her head, out of the window and into the sky, where clouds, once again, were forming into floating mountains.

They sat together in the faux Renaissance Parlour with its multi-coloured ice-creams and skylight frescoes and winds of change. Nina wasn't sure she knew a 'Tommy,' or who he might be, but he had the right name. After ten minutes with Aunt Merry you could see some elements of the younger girl in her: still assertive, mildly opinionated, with strong convictions and, if you knew her well, a kind heart. Her aunt and mother had followed very different careers, but now they were older, with more time to discover a new side to themselves and both with property and savings, their parallel lives had started to merge.

"I'll pester him for more details… sounded wonderful, from what I recall... I was only half interested as I had then been occupied by Goethe's journey to Venice. Goethe makes one idle… I long to read his travels and then find myself falling asleep to his words… an impossible combination… but we will choose Florence, the thought of Venice makes me sleepy with lapping water and the bobbing of gondolas, the ups and downs of bridges and those shiny, worn cobbles, I'll nod off at every turn. Ha!" Aunt Merry stifled a yawn and recovered. "I'll have to book soon, you will do this with me won't you darling?" Pushing aside the teapot and empty ice-cream glasses, she reached out her arms and held Nina's cold hands, rubbing them to warm her.

"Watch your handkerchief, it's on the floor," said Aunt Merry looking across the table to the ground. "Is that your good-luck charm or are you going to tell me there's no such thing?!"

37

Nina smiled, slightly embarrassed, very intrigued and of course delighted; she was all these, so much so, she blinked back tears.

Aunt Merry and Nina descended the stairs and left by the far-right set of double glass doors. Nodding at the doorman, Aunt Merry was recognised as a regular patron or certainly the sort of woman who might very well frequent the halls of Fortnums. Nina's thoughts on the diverse clientele included ladies of all the old, global realms. Perhaps one who might sit on a fortune of gold coins, a former Tsarina of the crushed Empire; a lady who might just have celebrated her purchase of a rare, long-lost portrait by Rembrandt at nearby Christie's St James; a Duchess popping in to order her groceries and to send a hamper to foreign cousins.

The streets and people of Piccadilly appeared like common chaos, having left the sparkle and gold glamour of Fortnums. The large ground-floor windows, usually a great attraction, were currently being dismantled. St Valentine hearts, chocolate boxes and champagne were making way for illustrious Faberge-styled eggs, suspended on yellow ribbons for the Easter display. The wild, grey outdoors, a human wilderness, was a great disappointment after having felt so bright and close to colour and touchable sun, but all was not lost, for Aunt Merry's offer stayed real and true. They walked to the church of St James' Piccadilly, where a meagre market was selling leather purses and bags, postcards and posters, sausage baps and noodles.

Inside the church, at the entrance, two wardens were making brass and grave rubbings whilst the third tried to guide a couple of confused Chinese tourists around the highlights of London using their oriental travel book. Aunt Merry went straight to the church noticeboard, whipping a pen and notepad from her bag she started to jot down various events she might attend, humming and chattering as she went, as if to narrate to the conscience on her shoulder. There was 'a book club,' 'a quartet giving a lunch-time concert,' 'an evening of meditation and relaxation,' 'Romantic duets,' 'poetry recitals as chosen by The Academy School,' 'three plays by Shakespeare in an afternoon,' 'African-American spiritual folk songs from a reciprocal church in Alabama,' 'The Piccadilly Chamber Music series.' Running her mythical diary through her head, 'yes, she'd do that,' 'no she couldn't make this, but could try,' 'no she wouldn't do that, not her thing,' 'she might stay for that' etc. She admired the London church for its diversity. It certainly wasn't like this at the Winchelsea church and a far cry from the kind of structure of her own church days. The multifariousness of London's churches was overwhelming, much like the great city itself which could never be fully accomplished for it was always metamorphosing into something else; once again evolution and theology would find themselves entwined in the same sentence, although this time with joyous merit.

The clock tower of St James' pealed three bells and, with a long hug, Aunt Merry and Nina parted. Her aunt was to stay the night in her St Martins Lane flat, with a view to renting it over the Florence period. The church of St Martin-in-the-Fields had a choir singing at 6pm followed by drinks in the crypt. Aunt Merry found wandering over the worn 17th and 18th century tombstones with a glass of red wine that had not been blessed at the Eucharist slightly peculiar. It was yet another challenge to her churchly background. Next she'd pop to a Covent garden trattoria, sit at her corner table and make pencil sketches on her paper napkin of the restaurant's guests. There was one regular customer whom she believed to be a re-incarnation of Winston Churchill. He nursed a fat cigar, which he tapped but didn't smoke; had a bald head, beady sharp eyes and a propensity for generous quantities of expensive alcohol.

Aunt Merry had told Nina to have the faith of a child, and to expect to travel early April. "Keep the month clear, my dear!" were her final words as she'd walked back to the hard pavement and stern traffic of a rushed and dirty road.

Nina's walk back to Charing Cross took her to St James's Square. The gates were locked, so on tiptoe she peered over the black railings like an inquisitive child from The Selfish Giant, wondering why this patch of cleansing air and space should be closed to the public. Most people would be indoors, in shops or uninterested at this time of year. From her position she viewed the short winter grass, the tidied plant borders, the clumps of neat snowdrops and the purple and yellow crocuses with their prized saffron centres, sown, supposedly randomly, but more likely very deliberately, beneath the spread of London's old plane trees, still tightly closed against the cold. In one of the evergreen bushes at the side of the square came a mechanical staccato sound, then long, honied notes of birdsong. Nina listened with a tight ear. She could not see the bird but the tune touched her pockets of memory. Her grandmother had once owned a small, round portable toy cage and inside sat a mechanised bird on a perch. She would wind it up using a long key and the little bird would tweet and twitter and move its tiny beak and sing, just as this bird did now. She had not heard a sound like it since. When she was five she'd taken the little caged bird out into the garden, when everyone was busy eating a large Sunday roast, to sing to the real birds nesting in the garden hedgerows. Not one bird sang like this tiny, nondescript, melodic bird. She would wind it up and watch it sing: sing its little heart out, full of joy and pain. She wanted to release the bird, but there was no latch or key or any method of opening the hard-wired cage and anyway it wasn't real. She couldn't give it the chance it was crying for. Its wings were useless but its song, its song would have made the last fledging fly from nesting box to the life it was born to. Now here was this bird once again, but this time it was real and it was free, free to fly anywhere it wished: to follow the others or to find a place of its own or a mate of its liking, for whatever it chose, it existed.

Nina was beginning to feel a chill. She passed the

end of the Haymarket and entrances to the National Gallery. There was so much to do in London. No one day alike. In Trafalgar Square there was a little drizzle and no sign of a waving man; the handkerchief was pushed deep inside her inner pocket. At the station her train was delayed by eight minutes. She boarded a quiet carriage at platform six and was fixed to her seat by an extremely overweight gentleman who snorted when he turned the pages of his newspaper until he settled on the challenge of three crosswords. He left at Wadhurst. At St Leonards she was met by her mother's warm smile and a heated car. From station to home was long enough to pass on details of her afternoon with Aunt Merry. She did not tell Mrs Hurst of the songbird or ask her if she believed in fate or that she, Nina, had thought intermittently of the handsome waving man. Now she considered him *handsome*, she hadn't before. Someone, who in this city of many millions, seemed to her to have an alluring presence. This man was walking all over her mind and developing in character as he did so. Unintentionally she had made a detour to the post office on her way to Charing Cross. Was there a chance he might be there and remember her? By her design, yes. In reality, of course not. The notion seemed better in motion, than it did verbally. But she was so different to the Nina of last week. She was destined for Florence. A silly preoccupation such as this, and feelings that had not really touched her before, would soon fade away like the long middle-distance of a painting. This April the city of the Lily would be hers to explore, through the generosity and graciousness of her Aunt.

Nina's exhaustion soon began to wrap around her and form a tight headache. When a short silence ensued Mrs Hurst wittered away about Hazel Parsons, using a sharp, high-pitched voice to imitate her, and her narrow-mindedness and how she would just like to have nothing to do with her. Nina semi-listened with honest grunts and huffs and single words of conversational magic like, 'really?' and 'oh!' and longer ones to show she was listening but could add nothing: 'well that's how it is!' and 'she'll never change.' Mrs Hurst acted out her monologue while Nina added her odd phrases. She rested her elbow against the car-window and rubbed her forehead, trying to ease the dull ache. She'd reserved a place in her head for the coloured clouds of Fortnums' ceiling. Painted clouds were soft and dreamy, they floated carelessly, caressing sharp contours and blurring hard lines. They were not responsible for a winter's deluge or darkening days, they brought shadows and played with sunlight; they offered dimension and substance; they expanded the landscape of life, revealing its beauty and sheltering its brevity. This time the waving man did not enter her thoughts. She did not invite him in.

Hazel Parsons came from a family of school teachers and she had risen to the highest position of all, a school governor on the board of secondary schools in a catchment area that had now been disbanded. However, before that time had come, three schools had named their science blocks after her: The Parsons Science Lab. This piece of information always found its happy way into unexpected, longer dialogue, as if all her life stemmed from and revolved around these singular moments. She was pragmatic, which was a useful skill; sometimes far too abrupt and worst of all she still maintained a discernible air of disapproval, something she had mastered proficiently from many years in education. Hazel Parsons was one of those people who had skipped youth and moved straight into middle-age, for this was an age in which she could cleverly operate her imperiousness. However the authoritative manner she had inherited, would pass with her. After years of discussing children she had produced none of her own.

Mrs Hurst supported Nina's decision to leave her job at the paper, suggesting she wrote a letter of thanks, informing her editor a good month and a half before her departure and then request from him a letter of reference. Mrs Hurst, pleased she had guessed correctly, had bought Nina a travel-guide to Florence which had been clearly skip-read by her mother with various pages folded back and sections bending flat from their centre binding. There was so much art and architecture to see and beyond that lay what wasn't known by books: wandering at will, finding things for yourself with a simple plan of the city and a sense of determination and enthralment.

On the 6th of March Nina received a travel itinerary from Aunt Merry requesting she send her some details. She'd bought her the same guide as her mother had done, so she now had two similarly read-through Florence guidebooks. At the end of her hurried letter Aunt Merry mentioned a trip she had taken recently to the Marylebone Church on the Marylebone-Euston road. She had offered her skills as a counsellor in their therapy room, known as the Browning Room.

'So called' she added, 'because the poets Robert Browning and Elizabeth Barrett were married in this very church, I saw the commemorative chapel window. Then they eloped to Florence, where she later died, and is buried. Buried outside the city in the Protestant Cemetery. The Cimitero degli Inglesi, they call it! Add it to the list!' The use of exclamation marks revealed her level of growing excitement.

Nina was forming a wonderful trip in her head and secretly hoped Aunt Merry would not feature in every one of her Florentine trails, although Nina knew she was with a woman who made things happen and chances appear. There was something wonderful in the mixture of knowing a little and knowing nothing of what was to come. Whatever Aunt Merry thought she could guide, no matter how many gods gathered above and angels came singing, she couldn't write the future.

Part III

Arriving in Florence

High in the skies of Florence circled and squealed the second swoop of swallows; their warm, glossy-blue backs and long tail streamers rose to an unreachable breeze. The air-currents were pierced only by a skyline of magnificent, holy architecture, undaunted by the climb to Heaven. The advent of this flock was a nod to summer; long, warm late evenings lay in wait. The prosperous season was eager to stage love and ready to dote on lovers.

Aunt Merry and Nina's arrival in May was a month later than originally planned. Why does everything take so long? April had escaped Aunt Merry. She'd spent most of the thirty days in a complete fluster, double-booking her therapy sessions, mixing up her dates by inadvertently following an old desk calendar and thus becoming understandably confused by the early arrival of Easter. She had lost her diary under one of the many travel brochures covering her floor, and missed numerous calls from 'helpful Tommy,' who was booking the Florence hotel. For this journey she was not with a tour group and refused to allow Nina to help with 'arrangements.' Nina grew nervous at the prospect of travelling with a woman who at one turn seemed single-minded and entirely in control and at the other too spiritually attentive, afloat in her concern for saving others.

They'd flown early from an overcast, runway-grey London to Pisa, tinged in terracotta and boasting a marbled old city and wealth of history. They would envision nothing of Pisa but shiny posters and plastic souvenirs. The airport might have been labelled anything Italian. They were hurried through the ubiquitous environment of tunnels, corridors and systems; there was something in the rapidity of the Latin language and the warm, dusty foreign atmosphere that encouraged them to move at haste. At arrivals they were cordially met by an overly large chauffeur, his physique resembling the leather driving-seat in which he habitually lounged. The paper-board he held bore the name 'Nina.' Aunt Merry had insisted they use Nina's first name: "It sounds Italian, well half Italian!" She felt pleased to have thought this through, "best we start off on the right foot." Savino, the driver, had podgy fingers, a tanned face and rumpled appearance but with one smile he seemed twice as pleased to greet his customers. He took all four bags, tucking one under each arm, sticking them neatly to his flesh, then preceded to roll one in front and one behind, prompting the first of Aunt Merry's remarks on Italians to be, "Italians are so... dexterous," and then she said "the pasta here will be different...it'll keep us going longer!" She took pride in her astute observations.

They followed him like faithful disciples to a black car, amongst hundreds of black cars parked at obscure angles. It took twenty minutes or more to squeeze and successfully manoeuvre the car around a thoroughly haphazard and disorganised car-park. Protruding objects and narrow spaces caused the two women to instinctively inhale sharply.

Savino drove like the wind, speeding up to red lights and thumping a heavy foot on the brake, tapping in agitation at the indignation of having to wait. He treated sharp corners and round-abouts like minor road ailments he intended to skip and bumped joyfully over pot-holes and speed-bumps as if he meant to shake some fizz back into a flat soda. Aunt Merry agreed with herself, there must be a televised football match pending and he needed to make it home, lest the team miss his vocal support.

"Calcio?" she asked, and like a true Italian he gesticulated wildly, this time taking his hands off the wheel and eyes off a perilous road and junction for one long minute and smattering the air with a selection of lyrical words joined to long vowels. It was of little meaning. Nina understood basic words and several phrases; in an idle and uncommitted month before their departure she'd taken an intensive language course. To Nina's comprehension Aunt Merry could add more substance, but at present she suffered from an ear infection brought about by high altitude and the pressurised steel cabin of an aeroplane.

Italians did not like to wait, not for traffic, not for food, not for an espresso, not for anything. Aunt Merry still believed in the distinguishing features and qualities of a culture and that the psyche of

Britishness was defined by patience and tolerance. *They* were virtues much prized and seldom found "amongst our European cousins and beyond." She had whispered courteously and in moderation, (she would be mildly deaf for three days before her ears cleared) "queuing and waiting is one of our English idiosyncrasies, though nowadays so many people expect everything straight-away, they really are missing out on the feeling that follows anticipation and becomes reward." She must have been thinking of something specific, her logic was a little 'off-piste.' Football was the life-force for so many nations, and this man was not going to miss his share of the action, but he was going to miss out on a tip. Aunt Merry had pulled out her envelope labelled taxi tips and reduced the notes by a third. Despite her first impression of his helpfulness, she rested on her second impression: "the Italians certainly do test one's nerves."

If Aunt Merry had considered, from her English oak desk in Winchelsea, she was going to blend into the Florentine picture as naturally as Leonardo puts his skilful brush to the subtle graduation of tone and colour, then she was very much mistaken.

It would take Aunt Merry and Nina more than a few days to become accustomed to each other's personalities and the early close proximity would be trying. In over a week their ears would become accustomed to the lilt and tempo of the Tuscan accent. The nuances of language and custom, style and distinction would remain a barrier between

Nina and the Florentines but she knew her role as tourist, and in good time she would delve deeper beneath the surface of the city than many of the impressionable young women it had previously enchanted.

The castellated hotel, entitled Antica Colonne on via di Morelli was once the family home of a prestigious banking family: the Morelli. This imposing edifice towered over the banks of the Arno and entry to it was permitted through a wide, embossed wooden gate. The body of the building comprised solid slabs of scarred stone symbolising its history of security and grandeur, having once enticed and repelled the incumbents of the city. The hotel sat conveniently within a local district of what Nina would describe as 'realness,' the main sites and a stretch of popular water. A short bridge led to further churches across the brown, fast-moving River Arno.

"Perfetto!" Aunt Merry had cried on seeing her home for the next few weeks. She felt pleased Tommy had seen her as a woman of such discerning taste. Quick to judge the glory of Antica Colonne's prominent position and its façade, the interior did not disappoint. In fact, it amazed and enlightened both travellers. Throughout the hotel stood graceful statues of marble, carved figurines in bronze and simple biblical scenes painted in egg tempera on poplar wood, in gilded frames. The burnished mirrors, almost as high as the ceiling, reflected the unique and personal collection, selected by the old financiers. Some of the more fractured pieces were dated as early as the 13th century.

Large white lilies in bulbous glass vases filled the hallways and a clean, soft-sandstone coloured oil-wash climbed the walls to a white, foliage-patterned cornice. Nina stood in awe, copying the movements of Aunt Merry, straining her eyes and extending her neck like an inquisitive ostrich. She wanted to examine everything closely yet was overcome by the opulence. From the far-right corner of the ground floor a hotel receptionist with black, thin-rimmed glasses and dyed flame-red curly hair, had spotted their arrival. She watched with pride as the Italian splendour soaked their senses. Perhaps it had been a while since she had seen the effect of her native Florence triumph over the English tourist. Nina had tried to hold back some of her astonishment but like asking a cat to curb its curiosity, it was impossible. From day one she had simply wanted to fit in as much as she could, but she could see too that from day one it would very difficult indeed.

They were too early to check in, "mi dispiace signore, the room t'is not ready, we can take bags, maybe you like to sit at la terrazza and we come call you." She spoke a non-perfect English mixed with Italian in a bouncy accent and made Aunt Merry believe her own Italian to be perfectly fluent. She understood more by tone and gesture. A sympathetic slant of the head and a dimple from the signorina implied there was a resolution to the immediate issue. Aunt Merry's ears were still weak but the spoken Italian was loud and clear. Nina replied, "grazie" and smiled.

Aunt Merry was unconcerned. She had already spotted an open church beside the hotel, Basilica di Santa Trinita. "If I've learnt anything on my travels to Italy, it's to grab the chance and see a church when it's open, because it may not be open again for another week!" Leaving their luggage with the concierge and accepting the offer to refresh themselves, Aunt Merry and Nina quickly washed off their journey and went out into the heat of the day.

It was dark and cool inside the church which boasted over twenty chapels. They wandered in silence and paused together at the most popular and celebrated chapel, that of the Sassetti family. Here, in the company of several other visitors, their heads immersed in guidebooks and leaflets, they admired the well-preserved 15th century fresco cycle depicting the tales of St Francis. It was executed by the famed artist Ghirlandaio and commissioned by the rich banker Sassetti. The kneeling donor and much of Florentine society peered down upon them as Nina thumbed through her own guidebook. 'Yes' thought the pious, kneeling patron in his long, red robes, 'you are reading about me: an affluent, influential figure, well-connected and much-admired by my compatriots. I am a benefactor to the most revered artist, I am an honest servant to God, I associate myself with St Francis, one of the most venerated religious figures.'

Aunt Merry preferred to trace the stories by sight rather than reading literature on the chapels of the church. Nina was torn, she wanted to understand what she saw and also to absorb her surroundings naturally and casually, without the concern for an open book and a printed lecture. Aunt Merry, taking a quiet moment, lit a small candle and glided around the church in perfect serenity, she seemed completely at home, at ease and, with her poor hearing, in a separate and delightful world. The warm ambience and the peace of the Florentine church, alongside the Antica Colonne, seemed to colour her complexion.

They returned an hour later to the hotel to find their suite a rather formal yet enchanting space. Aunt Merry threw open the window to the main bedroom, overlooking the river and a gentle breeze warmed the inside air. Standing back, she viewed a pink palazzo with green shutters and then behind, the dome of Santo Spirito, its white cross and tall bell-tower drew her eye upwards into a pale light. The water level was low exposing the bank on the far side. Yelps and cries of young people dangerously prostrating themselves on the buttresses of the nearby bridge could be heard, as they foolishly played precarious games, ignoring the currents and unpredictable swell below. From left to right a series of arched and modern bridges spanned the river's girth and the tiled roof of the famed Ponte Vecchio was just visible.

Both women relished the wonder of living in one popular district and yet seeking sight of another. Aunt Merry's room with its four-poster bed had a large wooden dresser with deep drawers, a sidetable with a bowl of fruit, tall bedside lamps and a small rug with a pair of simple slippers awaiting tired feet. There was an entrance area with more storage and clothes space, a fully-stocked tea-table and tea-chest with a sugar bowl and wrapped biscotti; a bay window, designed as a daybed with fat cushions and wispy white drapery led to a large marbled bathroom with all the modern-day facilities including a curtain across the bath and a heated-towel rail. Nina's room was adjoining Aunt Merry's with one window as opposed to two and a large mirror reflected the tight space.

Aunt Merry fell into a deep sleep minutes after resting her exhaustion into the feathered duvet. Nina unpacked her belongings speedily. She blew her hair from her forehead, ready to rest, yet acutely aware of new sounds and the smell of wood and bees-wax polish, A long day had already passed and with an extra hour ahead it still seemed to turn slowly. She sat on her bed and tested the mattress by bouncing up and down. It was from here she watched an envelope slide underneath the room door and she jumped up to receive it. It was addressed to Nina on hotel stationery: Antica Colonne, Via di Morelli, Firenze. She frowned at the hand-writing and tore open the envelope; instantly regretting her haste knowing she should have done this with more style. She hadn't yet located a paperknife; it was the sort of hotel that would have one.

Dear Ms Nina and Ms Smith

Please come join us for drinks on la terrazza at 6pm.

We're two ladies from Texas, regrettably leaving tomorrow. We've been in Florence for two weeks. Should like to say hello to you all before we go back to the States.

Kind regards

Evelyn and Paddy

Nina placed the invitation on the bedside table beside her dreaming aunt and returned to her bedroom. She drew the heavy curtains, a slant of light at the top refused to be shut out. She pulled a thin quilt over her legs, a cool breeze with a dusty scent encircled the room and the day suddenly caught up with all her stimulated senses. A wave of tiredness became overwhelming and within minutes she fell asleep.

By the time they arrived at the terrazza, a small party was in progress. Both ladies were offered a glass of prosecco from a large tray; the tiny bubbles popped on the surface and up along the stem of the glass. It tasted sweet and fizzy; a sparkling sip of the Italian wine signalled a switch from a long, public afternoon into a sophisticated private evening. Furthermore, the sweeping view from the terrazza was a privilege available only to the hotel client. Aunt Merry and Nina stood side by side in awe. "Wow," said Nina, "what a view!" Both were transfixed by sun-warmed, red rooftops and the perfect curves of Brunelleschi's great Duomo. Stretching into the far distance were the high, forested hills, their wispy layers of green against a pale blue sky. The Duomo was particularly splendid and dominant; the pulsing heart, a wonder and symbol of the city, reflecting and diffusing the beauty of Florence.

The quick effect of crisp Italian wine upon the tongue of a British guest was embarrassing in its decibels. Fast-flowing from a far corner, a man spoke loudly and animatedly, unaware of his echo and the awkward contrast of his modern accent upon a relatively timeless scene.

"Oh well… this is our fourth visit to Florence in two years, practically know the place backwards. Although… somehow managed to get a bit lost today looking for some wine-bar… turns out it's not where I thought it was... you know from last time… when we were… Any how! Love it here, just love it… couldn't stay anywhere *but* here…" The small tubby man pointed a finger to the ground to indicate the hotel. He continued on short breaths, "took a trip to Fiesole the other day… funny little place… really all the joy's in the journey, winding up these streets with greenery on either side. Reminds me of… er… oh what's the place?" He turned and looked across his shoulder for what must have been his wife. She looked very similar in build and colour as he, although the tubby man had adopted a voice-level passable for two people. She sat in a zipped silence, the type reserved for churches and libraries.

His lady companion, Marjorie, looked thoroughly bored; bored with her husband and bored with the sight of more terracotta. She sat with her back to the view of church spires, wonky rooves and juxtaposed houses and stared into a short distance of no merit: the hotel drainpipes. It seemed the impactful 'Duomo' no longer held for her the impact it provoked in a newcomer. She looked peevish and critical, and if nothing good could come from her pursed, lined lips then maybe nothing should be encouraged from them. Her eyes seemed tired of… what exactly: of every noticeable and unique intricacy of Florence? She could be enlightened no more by this wonder and that wonder and the marvel of this and the marvel of that.

"Marjorie, luv," shouted the tubby man with half a crisp in his mouth, "er… what did Fiesole remind us of?" Had he not seen this face of hers a thousand times before? And yet his zest and vibrancy still seemed to want to pursue her waspish attitude. Marjorie didn't want to respond to her name; she looked blank, to raise an eyebrow was a considerable effort, but she did this anyway. Her exuberant husband was talking to one of the Texan women, therefore it invited a twist of the head. As she lifted her back to shrug off his question, her hand reached out for another prosecco from a tray of freshly filled glasses as if it were her slim suitcase coming off the carousel at the airport. She had swift and nimble fingers and was in need of stimulation.

"No... we can't remember... well kind of a Florentine Cotswolds, Ha! Without the sheep and the stone walls and the fields of hay and what not." The Texan woman struggled to understand the man with his funny British accent and his penchant for chattering with a mouthful but she nodded amiably enjoying the vivacity of his quaint British tone.

Marjorie rolled her eyes. There was nothing her dearly beloved could say that she had not heard before. Every tale and anecdote were recited in the same silly, juvenile fashion. Every place they'd visited was always compared to some other place they had visited. Life for her seemed to have lost its charm while he delighted in making loose travel connections, if somewhat stretched and fantastical ones.

"I remember now... got it... Villa San Michele... fabulous view over the city... yes got it... Marjorie... Villa ... San... Michele." He repeated it for Marjorie, almost insisting she make a note. "You haven't been? Well next time..." The Texan woman hadn't spoken but the man, on seeing her open expression, assumed she had. He being the ardent adventurer, had been so clever in finding out the secret destination, could not imagine an American could possibly have found it. The Texan woman left him to his crisps and nuts as he signalled for more prosecco.

"Welcome ladies... you must be Nina," the Texan lady said to Aunt Merry who shook her head.

"No, no I'm Merry and this is Nina," said a happy Aunt Merry. Nina smiled. She commented on the fine evening light and the panoramic view. It was captivating to watch the clouds float aimlessly overhead like large white nests with streaks of purple and pink and in contrast to hear the street cries and bustling traffic below. It reminded her she was standing, and sleeping, somewhere high above the ground and far beneath the sky: a height and culture of new existence.

"How lovely of you to throw a party up here... we only arrived this morning!"

"Well... we come all this way and I said to Paddy it would be a fine thing to do... sorry it's our last night... but it's been swell here... an awesome city. Full of surprises... oh excuse me... I was expecting a package before I left." Evelyn put a hand on Nina's shoulder in a friendly gesture and encouraged them to mingle, then she scuttled out.

Nina surveyed the terrazza. At the edges were flowering tubs and olive trees neatly potted in ornamental gravel and slate and already bearing the black fruit. There was a mother and her son of about eighteen. They were sitting at a table mumbling words back and forth between each other; hers in a slightly cross and irritable tone, moving her mouth very tightly; he listened and added monosyllabic answers and whiney sentences. Nina remembered the days her mother and sister faced the same difficult predicament; a series of questions followed by terse and blunt responses. After having been such a chatty child, there was a long period of quietness before her sister finally began to interact and unfold. When at last she did, it had helped the three women in their close relationship and although today she was still reticent, she had moved on in great strides, sometimes better than Nina had, especially in recent years.

Aunt Merry also scanned the party; she picked out small groups of talkative people, their bubbly conversation dancing with stories, and laughter spilling into the air as happily as the wine swilled around their mouths. She could grasp the odd word or phrase; it was mostly English, laughter seemed a universal language. A few Italians and Spanish were pleased to have found their sort. Then she spotted a large, bent figure dressed in a black suit, like a broad shadow. He had round glasses and thin curly hair. Feeling in a courteous and therapeutic mood, a state of mind she could always use on approaching new people, Aunt Merry advanced toward him and Nina followed.

"Hello, I'm Merry and this is Nina… we arrived today… you look a little lonely… mind if we join you?"

"If you wish…" It seemed to ache his jaw to utter the three words.

"Lovely here... just splendid... we said so when we arrived... yes we'll be very happy here." Aunt Merry expected a reciprocal agreement but she received no such accordance. Surely there must something she could find that would unite them; they were staying in the same hotel and admiring the same breath-taking vista. "I do like names... do you have one?" she asked searching his glum face for some elevation.

"Yes, I was given one... Serge... S.E R.G.E." said Serge in a polite and ordinary tone; it was too quiet for Aunt Merry who had to ask again. This surprised Serge, his bushy eyebrows lifted up to his hairline which in turn amazed his feathery curls. He looked like the sort of man who was never asked the same question twice but he managed it ordinarily, without rudeness. It was rare for Serge's features to move from the seemingly fixed position they occupied; being so sullen and dismal, vitality seldom trickled through his veins.

"Oh... right... I shan't be taking notes... if I might say you look a little lost... a little sad... have I broken your train of thought? If so I'm sorry... I'm feeling... how to put it? A bouncy version of my usual self." Aunt Merry tapped her glass, not meaning to attract a waiter but somehow she did, and suddenly she had two men by her side. Nina stood behind her aunt, feeling a little embarrassed and self-conscious and longed to be camouflaged into the background, out of sight.

"You may say whatever you like," said Serge, partially interested to know what this woman might say next.

"Well isn't it just wonderful here!"

"I fear, Madame… you have an excitement and enthusiasm I cannot match… I am French… wherever we go we are disappointed. I find the sun, I want the dark… I see a view, I want a room… I'm on a terrace, I want to walk a street… it is my way."

"Oh are you a painter… can we see your work?" Aunt Merry would not let go of her wonderings, "you don't sound French at all…unless it's my ears?"

"Alas, I'm just that… a French painter… making my way across the cities of Italy… I do not exhibit."

"Well Florence must be marvellous inspiration for you… so much to see… we will be doing the galleries and churches." Serge had noticed Nina, the antithesis of himself. Her eyes were wide, reflecting a hovering cloud or soaring bird, her ears open, catching an urban symphony or the skylight melody. From the eye and ear straight into the soul; it was spirit, vigour and force to her, it was melancholic interpretation to Serge.

"I think, Madame, I must retire… I'm rather sleepy, but first I will take a walk down by the river… goodnight to you."

"Oh goodnight Serge... maybe see you at breakfast?"

"Perhaps Madame." He bowed out and stumbled his heavy weight inside.

Aunt Merry turned to Nina. "Oh dear, what a sad man... and he paints too... I might like to pick up a souvenir at some point. It's so difficult to help and encourage such lonesome men. They say very little and are permanently downcast... and there's never any point in telling them how lucky they are... they'll only dig a deeper hole... like a crestfallen King. They are encouraged but discouraged and disenchanted by enchantment. What a terrible mix!"

Aunt Merry and Nina sat at a table and breathed in the high, luxuriant air. There was the chink of glasses and a soothing hubbub; they felt lulled by the atmosphere: art, wine, palazzo, view. And out there, in the deep city were old and new stories to be told and expectations to be fulfilled and the senses to be indulged.

Part IV

Walking tour

Tossing and turning, Nina slept uneasily that first night: over-excited and slightly dizzy. She was eager to see the great sites of Florence, to finally explore the hidden treasures of the city, to let names and words and symbols come to life before her. And for herself, an inspiring change. She thought it was here she would be enlightened and relax into a new personality, but this was an awful lot to expect of Florence.

Aunt Merry had clearly slept soundly and was refreshing her face with a series of creams and oils when she and Nina spoke. She had been awake some time, had passed a delightful hour in the company of her guidebook on Florence and had pin-pointed the places she intended to see and made a sub-list of extras. Her customary six hours sleep a night could be maximised into a good four hours sightseeing a day.

Over the course of their first week it was 'essential' and 'necessary' to do a thorough walking tour of the many highlights of Florence. Nina watched her aunt use these words quite wisely and deliberately and she realised immediately it was more about her aunt's health and ability. Her energies would be at their best in these early, fresh days. Later she would lessen her pace, though not her enthusiasm. Anything she felt had been hurried or underdone, she would re-do with the calm tempo of one who had purposefully reserved ample time for such pleasures, or else she would suggest Nina, who would not need encouragement, should go visiting alone. Thereby Aunt Merry could live an experience through the eyes and energies of one much younger and thus imagine herself there in soul if not in person.

Her aunt stated she was not an art historian, but she was most definitely an art appreciator. They would not do too much, although at the same time they would not miss anything, they must stroll like dedicated tourists but stray like detached travellers, both dutiful in their respect of the great city. It was an entirely mis-interpretation of 'balance.' Nina loved her plan, because she saw no balance in her theory so anything could happen, just as it should be allowed to.

At the hotel they took, what Aunt Merry described as 'a dry breakfast;' thin, crispy toast with book-leaf slices of pale-white cheese and bitter-black coffee served in small cups. While her aunt hummed to a tune of abstract music that drifted on the tail-end of a breeze, over the balcony, into her ears and onto her tongue, Nina skimmed through her own guidebook. At last! She was looking forward to finally meeting those spectacular images, so poorly photographed and scrupulously analysed by the dull book. She decided to refer to it very occasionally, study the streets from the hotel's own free pianta (map), providing an enlarged area of the main attractions. She'd not miss the surroundings by having her head stuck inside printed materials. She packed a camera, wishing it wasn't so heavy and awkward.

And so, as it came to pass, all became real. They donned their most comfortable shoes, slipped maps and guidebooks into their bags and with happy strides stepped out into unknown streets. They weaved their way around sharp corners and foreboding facades, along slippery dark alleyways and popped in and out of patches of sunlight, hopping from charcoal shades to bright whites in a patchwork of trails. The first destination was the Uffizi. Their pre-booked, timed-entry tickets saved them hours of queuing. Aunt Merry quite liked a queue, it was a chance to meet a stranger, and since they, the stranger that is, were sharing this common ground, this like-minded destination, they might as well be engaged in conversation. Nonetheless, they passed by the ever-expanding and lengthening line of less well-organised tourists and went in. Aunt Merry could feel an ounce of smugness creep around her mouth and into her eyes, and fearing Nina might see it she hurried on ahead. Nina was too busy absorbing the atmosphere, the physicality of the world growing around her. She followed a little behind, obediently in step but stubbornly in thought; capturing this new scenery was like unravelling a gift.

Fumbling with a gallery map Aunt Merry

whispered, "I'm going to view Giotto's altarpiece, 'The Ognissanti Madonna,' and we must take a look at Piero della Francesca's portraits of 'The Duke and Duchess of Urbino'… the most hooked nose in history!"

She puffed knowledgably yet excitedly, "why these paintings are so close at hand, it's like walking into a room to meet your idol!"

First impressions of paintings were just as important as meeting people for the first time, and she'd come all this way. She couldn't be disappointed, not with real art, hanging on the walls, displaying its story and history. However, knowing how a church sermon could prolong itself, every visit too must have its timings. Aunt Merry had put a limit on her choice of paintings to view. She wanted to sail through the gallery rooms with clarity and certainty.

Nina gazed at the decorated ceilings and walls, and the long glass corridor. Her aunt continued to chatter in a soft voice, forcing Nina to lean in closer to listen and thus take her full attention. Aunt Merry could see Nina's feet and mind longed to go wandering in harmony, and yet she did not want to lose her niece. Once all those other tourists got inside it would be an impossible, crowded place, bustling and noisy and disorganised; a messiness not conducive to Art. Art, like the church, should be nurtured, preferably, she considered, in a calm and sheltered environment; it encouraged inwardness, thoughtfulness, contemplation and quiet observation. Although, occasionally in contradictory mood, Aunt Merry understood in order to fill churches you must have tolerance and this she had always heralded as a valuable asset, on a par with patience.

"Then I'll work my way to the Botticelli room, 'The Birth of Venus' is a must... there's the ancient roman statue, 'Spinario' the boy removing a thorn from his foot... I long to see the serenity of Raphael's 'Madonna,' and the depiction of Leonardo's 'Annunciation,' an image I never tire of reading... then, here," she pointed to the last star of the map, "Michelangelo's 'Holy Family,' it's rather unconventional, but a must-see for its unusual round 'tondo' form." Aunt Merry stood back and sighed; she waited for Nina to respond. Nina remained quiet.

"And that will be it!" said Aunt Merry, gleefully.

After one magnetic hour drawn to the masters of art, fascinated by their work and the impact and inspiring influence of one generation upon the other, they said farewell to the Uffizi.

With self-confidence and above all feeling uplifted, they exited and stood for a moment under the shaded colonnade. They paused for a breath of warm, dusty Florentine air. Nina closed her eyes slowly in a long blink, soaking up the past she had just lived in, selecting and condensing these extraordinary visions into the pockets of her mind. Then, opening clean fresh eyes, and close on the heels of her aunt, they together pushed on through the Piazza della Signoria.

Her aunt, although slightly breathless, liked to keep a commentary going as they moved in and out of the straggling awe-struck tourist and their flock.

"I'm accepting, but…" her aunt hesitated, "a trifle sorry these famous statues are now housed in museums. I'm looking at a perfectly wonderful statue of David," she pointed to her right in a sweeping gesture, "but I know it's a copy… the originals are housed inside museums around the city… David's in… the… The Accademia." She said it so amusingly, so casual in tone and yet she was also thoroughly disappointed. Did she expect an apology? Nina wanted very keenly to say, 'it's not *my* fault.'

When Nina was younger, she remembered her little sister used to go about the house exclaiming 'it's not my fault.' Not rudely, just matter-of-factly. If it was raining, if the cat was meowing, if the clock was wrong, if they were out of milk, it was not *her fault*. No-one ever said it was, the phrase had just caught her tongue and she used it for everything until eventually, when she'd learnt new things to say, it was swallowed up and disappeared. And here, very suddenly, Nina thought how much she would like to use it, but it was childish and out-dated. She'd rather explain,

"But they'd be ruined by pollution... weather and maybe vandals, if they were just left outside... it makes sense," said Nina. It was obvious to her these sculptures should be protected and safe, surely her aunt could see that. "This way," she continued, "we see the figures in-situ and the originals stay safe indoors. Florence would be empty without its outdoor copies."

"Yes... yes, I know... like I said The Accademia... The Bargello," read her aunt, leafing through her guide book and checking the bookmarked pages. "Now let's press on." Nina was pleased her aunt had made peace with such a conundrum: wanting to see the real thing and wanting to see it in place.

The May heat was escalating and a hot wind swirled around the square, a few swallows squealed overhead but they were gone before Nina had a chance to catch a curved black wing. As they passed by the quiet and shaded curves of Orsanmichele, a dank drain odour wafted around their noses. "Yuk," said Nina and her aunt held her nose. Nina stopped to read aloud, "Or-san-michele, Orsanmichele, originally a grain market... the statues in the niches represent the patron saints of each of Florence's major guilds."

"*These* are copies too," lamented Aunt Merry, with a sour face, she had taken a gulp of gutter air and spied an open-air market, both at the same time. The sight of her contorted expression made Nina laugh. She snapped a photo.

Nina worried Aunt Merry was going to put a damper on their trip by becoming irritable and aggravated. Maybe, just maybe, she would be better sitting on the hotel terrace, tucking into olives and wine and thinking what a wonderful place she had found; what a wealth of culture there was in Florence and how supremely fortunate she was, but actually she was quite happy not having to involve herself in its public-ness. Nina thought back to Serge from the previous evening, but Aunt Merry was nothing like him.

Along the dark, narrow street of shops and passageways, they were assailed by the booming bells of the duomo, much closer and considerably louder than they had anticipated. "How wonderful!" they both cried in unison. Increasing their pace, leaving one sight of interest in expectation of another; discarding smells and shadows, they suddenly reached the bright square of San Giovanni. Face to face with the towering red, white and green cathedral, the sonorous calling of the campanile and the red-brick, herring-bone dome, the two ladies stood back and let the leading site of Florence soak their senses. Their gasps and sighs were drowned by its bellow. Their eyes were filled with colour and size. Dazzling, domineering, magisterial the heart of Florence summoned the visitor. When the last of the echoes was over, Nina took a minute to read a paragraph from her guidebook.

Nearby was The Baptistery and, wandering independently, they studied the East Doors, the panels Michelangelo had christened 'The Gates of Paradise.' Nina wanted to confer with her aunt but noticed she was deeply involved in a one-sided conversation with a poor sun-red French man. He could not understand her, but was being very polite about it. He was standing back attempting helplessly to take a photograph without a single person in it, while she, well it would have seemed to him, babbled, trying to explain that the panels were copies not originals.

"These panels, they're not real you know, they're copies. The originals are in the... the Museo dell' Opera del Duomo, it says here... Oh... oops," she said, catching the frown on his foreign forehead. "Now how do you say it... it's the same in every language!" she exclaimed, holding up her book and tapping the page and small-print, surely gestures were a universal language; he was not an Englishman nor, for that matter, an Italian.

Nina glanced at her aunt sympathetically; she was beginning to tire, her feet were sore and her mouth was dry, and Nina was certain this would lead to other complaints. Nina liked to fix the anxieties before they increased in number so she led her aunt slowly around the near side of the duomo. They stopped briefly but significantly to admire a large marble sculpture of the cathedral's architect, Brunelleschi. He was seated on a plinth set within two columns, gazing up at his triumphant building with the tools of his talent in hand. Nina followed his long, fixed stare, craning her neck, once again, to marvel at his masterpiece.

"Brava, brava… off we go!" cried Aunt Merry, still moving. Her spirits needed refreshing and her legs needed a rest because very soon, her 'feet would hurt' and 'her knee would ache' and she already felt faint and woozy. The crowds and the temperature and the dryness were affecting her.

Nina found a solution to suit them both, a cool, corner gelateria and café, where she grabbed a free window table. Tiredness hit her and Aunt Merry was buoyed to the spot. They sat quietly, reading the café menu and sipping some tepid water Aunt Merry carried in a flask. A light, warm, city-scented breeze brushed across their bare arms and perspiration began to cool them instantly. Nina went to order at the counter. Her aunt had opted for a glass of rose and a sandwich of mozzarella and tomato, which seemed to come with a small salad and a handful of crisps as well. She was as she said, 'thirsty and famished' and on handing Nina her purse she lifted herself up to view the glass freezer of ice-creams, which must have been, 'well over twelve-feet long.'

"After that, I'm having one of those," she said, naughtily eying all the fabulous mixed colours of gelati with a glint in her eye. The great gleaming trays were churned in luxurious sweetness and each variety came with a wide paddle that spread its whipped thickness into a pot or a cone. Nina's mouth-watered. She was hypnotised by their tantalising allure and their seductive names, their coolness and the sweet joy they would bring to her parched tongue. What flavour-revelation was waiting for her, just lying there, waiting to be consumed. Italians could make everything sexy.

"Why there must be a hundred flavours... oh and what's that?" she said pointing at several little pots layered with sponge and cream and cocoa.

"Tiramisu," said a friendly owner, while he cleaned the glass freezer-front with a spray and cloth. "You like dis one?"

"Oh yes I like... *mi piace molto*... oh but Nina," she said looking between the two of them, she was worried his English and her Italian would not stretch to much more. There was always gesturing, she thought again. Yes, Aunt Merry was enjoying her mimes and motions. "Let's start with wine... *cominciamo a vino!*" she smiled and this, the Italian agreed was the very best answer to everything. He scampered into the kitchen, taking their order and delivering a delicious, very simple sandwich to the two exhausted ladies. Aunt Merry devoured hers, and drinking her first glass of light rosé as you might water from a fountain, she ordered a second.

Nina fiddled with her guidebook while her aunt sat contentedly. Her mind was racing with all they had seen. She pondered over the beauty of the artworks; the paintings, the great statues and the spectacular sights, and then she stopped thinking because thinking was as exhausting as walking and started observing: 'reading the story acted before you' her mother had said of observing. A young couple, in shadow of the duomo, were kissing; their arms wrapped around each other in a loving embrace. They were inseparable, as entwined as if they'd been sculpted that way and, most of all, totally unconcerned with the world around them. There she was, in one of the most romantic cities in Europe and here was something she had not found, something she had not felt. Not yet, or not ever; she didn't know. A negative jibe at her senses. Love was not in guidebooks or on sight-seeing tours, this you had to find yourself, if you could find it at all; maybe Florence might find it for her. She was being philosophical but a lot can be considered when you look about and observe. She wondered if anyone was watching *her*, after all the man with the handkerchief had picked her out. If she stayed in the café long enough, might someone see her inner loneliness. How would they describe her?

After half an hour, they paid the bill and chose a gelato, three ladles high. Aunt Merry chose hers by colour and made Nina take a photo claiming, "these are exactly the three colours I want to paint the bathroom: strawberry pink and hazelnut beige… and maybe this pale lemon or that custardy crema." She chose the lemon for zing.

Nina took a bitter chocolate sorbet, a pistachio di Bronte and a bright red raspberry. They'd freed their table to sit on some warm stone steps nearby, shaded by the café awning. The high sky was a deep blue with wispy stretched clouds; a half-moon was visible, hanging nimbly above the dome. Surely with a taste sensation such as this and a city as beautiful and as graceful as this, people must be in love all the time. Nina looked for the kissing couple, they had gone but she had seen them and she was pleased, a touch of love had licked the air.

Part V

To the Cemetery

A week of intensive tourism had taken its toll on Merry's energies and she had fallen victim to a disagreeably upset tummy and retired to her bed.

Without the daily companionship of her aunt, Nina felt secretly liberated. She did not feel too guilty, Aunt Merry was over the worst of her mild bug and had managed to attract the attention of two men of similar age who had recently joined the hotel. She had made her peace with Serge, whose mournful stance and melancholic look had intrigued her; he seemed so perpetually bored in a city so glorious. Aunt Merry, calling on him at breakfast when she was her most vibrant and talkative and, her face freshly made, had taken a delicate approach with him, having seen many confused and tortured souls in her lifetime. And yet with Serge it appeared he'd personally crucified himself and then stubbornly refused to be resurrected, and thus existed in some middle-land gloom. Nina pictured him with a dark grey cloud above his head where it lingered with its threatening pessimism. A glum, sour and dissatisfied man, he also brought with him a flavour of arrogance. Nina, who mentioned the subject to her aunt, thought he behaved in such a way as to make people believe he bore the arduous afflictions of a genius and was headed for sainthood, if only someone might bestow it upon him. In which case this assumption combined with the artworks of the city were reason enough for him to be in Florence. On the hotel's premises, Serge, Aunt Merry and Nina were now friendly and so familiar with each other to politely avoid contact whenever possible; Aunt Merry opting for the lift, Serge rising after midday and Nina darting her eyes in all directions and almost always finding a wonderful piece of decorative art to distract her. The behavioural language of polite evasion.

One morning Nina woke exceptionally early; the bells of six o'clock were calling across the city and the citizens would soon cast away sins and rejoice in prayer. She lay in bed with hands behind her head and watched the fresh sunlight filtering through the gap in the drapes highlight tiny particles of dust, dancing freely in the air and tickling about her nose.

Outside in the cool morning, the cooing of doves contrasted with the high-pitched squeal of swallows; the former felt homely, gentle and sympathetic while the latter's swift cry and eagerness willed the dozy sleeper to rise and climb out of bed, lest the enjoyment of the day be filled and polluted by more arrivals. Within the hour Nina was dressed. She scribbled a brief note to her aunt. She ran down the stairs, preferring the decorated descent over the claustrophobic lift. On each floor (there were six in total) she could stare and admire the artwork and sculptures and breathe in the aroma of the morning's new flowers, already neatly arranged in clear glass vases atop a marble mantelpiece or tucked into an old fireplace. There was the evocative morning smell of fresh bread and the distant sound of an already busy coffee grinder. Long-worded, operatic orders passed between hotel staff occupied with daily chores. The cycle of the day punctuated by regular hotel customs had begun at L'Antica Colonne.

Nina had decided in her sleep and confirmed on first waking, when it takes a few simple seconds to coordinate night-time and day, she'd take a walk to il Cimitero degli Inglesi, the English Cemetery. The idea gained momentum as a dormant seed waiting to be watered and brought to light. Her early wakening had confirmed a fine day. 'Yes, I'll do it, I *will* give the place time now, all the other destinations are complete. I can relax a little, walk less purposefully and give myself the luxury of time.'

Originally it was Aunt Merry who had made the suggestion of visiting Elizabeth Barrett Browning's grave in the cemetery on the outskirts of town but her aunt's malaise had softened her enthusiasm. Now, freed of her aunt's slightly tiring companionship, Nina had adopted the idea and made it her own objective. A strong desire, an angelic calling perhaps was urging her to make the trip today; 'sometimes the idea in your conscience is the counsel of an angel,' Aunt Merry understood this and Nina knew she would be pleased to let her go, to think it was for her, Nina, to be guided there. Now Aunt Merry was partially inactive and, on occasion, feeling the tired side of seventy, Nina would go alone and unburdened. But it would be for her will and not at the recommendation of another; the theory of a divine angel leading her onwards she'd treat with discreet circumspection.

Since the day of arrival Santa Trinita church had remained firmly closed. Nina had hoped to visit the chapels once again when she was less weary and more at ease. This morning, however, it was clearly open and many local Florentines, mostly very short, slightly plump ladies with rosary beads, were pushing and fumbling to get inside to pray, to cross their forehead in holy water and to confess sins. Nina stood back and then she crossed the street to let them pass, she suddenly felt like an interloper. She did not want to confuse her role as bystander with that of believer, for she knew well it was the frescos she wanted to view and not the religion she wanted to pursue.

She had memorised a route to the cemetery. A repetition of roads and backstreets, alleyways, piazzas and landmarks had made the trips about town much closer and this familiarity gave her an independent edge and confidence about the foreign city. Filtering through the streets and archways she passed il Cattedrale di Santa Maria del Fiore; the red, white and green flower of the city, possessor of Brunelleschi's great dome, soaring into a sky as deep and as blue as the ocean; commanding the skyline of Florence with an imperious and unimpeachable majesty. Already crowds had begun to gather, swarming like honey bees. Nina passed through more cobbled and darkened little alleys arriving at another wide and yet more subdued piazza, Piazza della Santissima Annunziata, home to the Catholic church of the same name and to one of the first sites that made Nina stop, sit and be saddened, Ospedale degli Innocenti. Both the church and this orphanage were arcaded with smooth, classically rounded arches and soft, cooling white walls.

Nina gazed upwards at the orphanage front to the glazed terracotta round cameos of babies wrapped in swaddling clothes on a blue background; she rested her legs solemnly on the steps beneath one of the slender columns. The roundels were by della Robbia, but she would have to remind herself of which one, Andrea or Luca? There were so many names and dates to remember, why could she not remember this? She did feel a bit faint and woozy, and searched for a biscotti in her inner pocket, one she'd grabbed from the bedroom tea table on the way out. Perhaps Nina had been moved this way since she'd arrived. Now, after viewing hundreds of stunning masterpieces - all those paintings, grand or intimate, the sculptures, small or large physical forms and the architecture of churchly splendour and rich vastness or more modest palazzi - a jumbled dizziness overpowered her. This sacred city of Florence appeared to exude an extraordinary energy, this time demonstrating its debt to human compassion.

Although Nina was not a mother, she was a woman

of great feeling and today her sensory impulses felt particularly sensitive. She imagined all her nerve endings to be acute and easily pained. This moment's pause at the orphanage seemed to take the breath from her voice and the energy from her limbs. She walked slowly to the end of the portico and peered at the rotating stone dish on which heart-broken mothers once placed the babes they could not afford to keep. Breaking the bond of birth, they delivered their child in anonymity to another to form its future with only a tiny memento, maybe a ribbon and a note 'mi chiamo Rosa.' The bell was rung and the stone was turned; the child was taken from them forever into the care of the hospital. What misery and grief under such a calm and gentle loggia. Was there a fountain of mother's tears somewhere close by, one that never dried? Would the dark interior bring relief and rescue? The exterior was designed with great architectural precision and balance in such an unbalanced world.

Nina's pensive thoughts were broken by the cries of school-children wending their way through the piazza, doubtless on a school trip to Brunelleschi's dome. She took a bite of an apple she'd brought; the pale juice was sweet. She placed the fruit on the top stone step of the first bay, beside the infant's entry, and left the square via a narrow alley. When she turned back, a collared dove had begun to peck at the apple and oddly she felt pleased that on those same sad steps a benefit might befall something, even if it was just a hungry dove, Aunt Merry would see a sign in it.

Arriving at the Cemetery island she found it surrounded by Monday's commuter traffic. A flume of frustrated cars coughed their way around Piazzale Donatello: this road encircled the raised, condensed graveyard. It was refreshing to see slim, pointed cypress trees, like green church spires connecting Earth to heaven. Nearby poplar trees rustled in a light breeze as if putti sang upon their branches. Nina made her way to the entrance at the far side and was fortunate to find the iron gates open and a sign proclaiming English Cemetery (Swiss Property). She wandered through, following a gritty path leading to a refined wooden gateway with plaques of poetical lines from the cemetery's most famous resident, Elizabeth Barrett Browning. Nina had tasted loneliness and loss and somehow, by being in a graveyard she felt absent from the world and thus would be entreated to think of the worlds in which these inhabitants once lived: a very diverse Florence. The city would have been shaped differently, housing another lifestyle and another way of being. In general, it was Art that survived much longer than people and was a setting for each generation to act out the scenes and stages of their life.

Nina, however, was not entirely alone, like sparrows at play, a little Italian chatter caught her ear. She could see the back of a tall man, one hand by his side, the other reaching to his inside pocket, where he found a dark-green handkerchief to brush his nose, he cleared his throat noisily. He was dressed in un-matching linen: cream-coloured jacket and green trousers. A panama hat sat softly on the top of his head, stirred only by his own movements. Solid and curved like a sculpture, standing with his weight to one side in contrapposto, no outside source could topple or ruffle him. For a split-second Nina thought she had seen him before. She had seen so many bodies in Florence but on a living one she had not lingered so long.

The other, much smaller man wore a cap and comfortable, shabby gardening clothes and was leaning on a rake. He took a heavy pull on a flask of water and mopped his brow with a soiled, rough glove. He was in profile and with a little idealising of his features in paint, his side-portrait might have rivalled the Duke of Urbino. He had a strongly defined nose and earthy skin, had he not been talking so animatedly between drinks, he would have maintained an uncanny resemblance to the Renaissance Duke but then again, Nina had seen so many faces in art: egg tempera on poplar wood, oil on canvas, frescoed wall, all faces were starting to blur.

The thread of conversation was something to do with *'acqua'* and *'fiori'* and *'il tempo,'* interspersed with verbs and terms Nina could not gather, but she wasn't there to listen. The taller man nodded his agreement, *'parlami lentamente'* he said. Nina knew these two words all too well; *'speak slowly,'* she had used them many times.

Nina had seen an image of Elizabeth Barrett

Browning's grave at her local library; the guidebook had been helpful only in its directions. She left the two men, who had not seen her, and continued a few steps on toward the central path. The scape of the cemetery was like the concept of a painting itself. The tall trees of fir, pine and poplar were the orthogonal lines giving height. The graduated horizontal graves, in their many forms and designs, were the transversal lines giving depth and the path, at the very centre of the gateway, led to the vanishing point. Each of these three elements gave perspective, they were a technical advantage to painting three-dimensional space onto a flat board. Nina had observed the clever use of it in many paintings; sometimes it was well-used and effortless, in other early works artists had struggled with their format and composition, confirming it was a much harder skill to master than originally thought. Nina contemplated her vision; it was very much a real space in which to stroll. She favoured wandering between the monuments, headstones, sarcophagi, Celtic crosses, tombstones, statues, and crucifixes, keeping mostly in the sun and only finding shade from an olive bush or marble shadow. Being the month of May, a mauve iris, speckled white and deep purple, grew slender among its thin reeds of leaf, there were not many open but enough to colour the shades of vibrant green grasses. Many of the headstones recorded members of the same family; small stones for babies; weeping angels, sculptured wreaths of flowers, broken columns, urns and vases, and simple flat slabs with ornate lettering and elaborate condolences. Here and there grew white rose bushes with spiky, thick thorns. In contrast, self-seeded Flanders poppies with their flimsy stems, bright splash of fresh, youthful red and fine, wrinkled petals bobbed innocently, and like Tommy on the Western front, they would be dead on the ground by the end of the day. Their seed would find soil somewhere new and root again in the graveyard wilderness.

She returned to the path and Nina smiled, for she recognised the ornate marble tomb immediately. Sitting prominently on six small columns with the initials E+B+B + 1861 with a round portrait relief. She had found the final resting place of Elizabeth Barrett Browning. Slightly startled, her moment was interrupted. Beside the tomb stood the tall man dressed in linen with shoes of brown leather and thin, black laces. He removed his hat in respect, revealing hair straight and thick with silvery flecks. He balanced himself mournfully on the shaded side of the grave. Close by grew a deep red rose, the top half lit by the sun. Nina always had the urge to smell a flower; irises did not have a fragrance but this rose had the potential to be as beautiful in softness and scent, as the sculpted tomb was in solidity and sensitivity. This tomb was both grand and humble; large enough to be recognisable yet restrained in decoration. It was difficult not to distract the gentleman but, considering she had come all this way and would not do so again, Nina felt she must go over and take a closer look.

"Hello there," said the linen man quietly. The soft

tone of his voice gently reflected the atmosphere of intimacy and calm; two souls drawn together in a single moment. He turned to face Nina with a warm, friendly face.

"Hello… um… B… Buongiorno," replied Nina.

"Buongiorno, I thought you might be English," he said without an ounce of irony, "have you come to visit Ms Barrett?"

"Yes to both," said Nina, "have you come a long way? I don't want to disturb you."

"Oh I come regularly, when I'm in Florence… which is usually about three months at a time." He paused and took a step forward. "I'm Arthur." He held out his hand to her but Nina was slow to respond, she'd been caught by some of the details of the grave she'd not seen from further away.

"Nina," she said, "I had a gerbil called Arthur once."

'Oh no,' thought Nina, angrily. As soon as the stupid words fell from her lips, she wished to retract them. Why had she said this, of all things? And now the embarrassment brushed over her cheeks, hot like a tempered rash. How could she retrieve this conversation?

"He was a very handsome gerbil," said Nina, feeling the situation twist into tighter knots.

Arthur gave an amused laugh. 'Goodness,' she thought, 'he's so elegant even his laughter is like a flurry of rain on a scorching day.'

"You look like a Nina," he said, smiling kindly.

'So he had looked at her,' thought Nina and, 'oh dear.' She felt he wasn't seeing her in the best light not in figure or in speech. She'd chosen a pretty Indian-print, lined skirt which was too hot for the increasing temperatures, as were the leggings she had needed that morning and now wished were not sticking the heat to her legs. She also wore a plain, light t-shirt and a soft, pink cardigan with a velvet edge sewn with thin, blue beads. It was a sensible urban outfit and cheerful too but nothing special and she'd been walking in it for over an hour in city dust; her shoes had lost their bounce too. Here she was as realistic and as natural as could be, meeting a gentleman within the backdrop of a graveyard. And, she thought, if this was not a chance to grab life and find beauty amongst the rested and peaceful, then where would be? Perhaps he had already swallowed such a thought. If a lady's poetry can link two minds then her shrine can make two meet.

"You sound English, do you speak Italian well?" Nina forgot immediately the sounds she had heard from him before.

"I'm half Italian, on my mother's side, Arturo she called me and my Italian is fluent – I just don't speak *horticultural* Italian… as you probably heard earlier when I was talking to Giorgio, the gardener. He always talks so fast – very Italian!" Arthur's eyes crinkled into a smile that looked easy and relaxed on his lightly tanned face. "My father was English. Sometimes I'm Art but that name doesn't work well in Florence. The place is full of Art." He smiled again; a phrase he was obviously used to saying and felt safe with.

Swallows cried overhead, probably only half a dozen; it was too high to see them. Their squeal diverted Nina's eyes while Arthur focused on her. He looked not like an artist squinting for form, but like a man who wanted to draw back the layers of her soul and to know this young lady for her confidence and wisdom and for her distinctiveness. It was unusual for him to meet such an attractive individual, to talk simply and freely and to begin a first meeting with new fervour. It was not until he'd seen Nina that he realised how much he loved colour in his life. He yearned to hold someone special and to love someone different, above all he'd already gathered.

"Well I've always been Nina… my sister's called Anneka and then I'm… oh never mind." She flapped her hand across her face as if a fly had confused her; nothing was there to muddle her words but there easily could have been; hatched flying ants were a favourite of dipping swallows.

"I'm here with my aunt, she's back at our hotel near the Arno." Why was she introducing people who weren't even there? She continued anyway.

"We've been here a week. My aunt, she's called Merry, is just recovering from a bug so I'm out on my own today, which is wonderful! It's my first time in Florence and I've really walked my feet off... I'm not complaining, I love it! It's the only way and there's so much to see and look at. We've done all the top spots, and to tell you the truth... I quite like the second week... less pressure. The main sites always demand to be seen first, and then people go home... but the second week is for exploring the lesser-known areas... that's what I'm doing now."

"And what's the third week for?" Arthur asked, fascinated.

"By the time the third week comes you are a proper Florentine... of course you know your way around without a map, you know which café to buy a pastry in, or where to buy a gelato before the children are out of school, you can do it twice a day – early afternoon or late at night, you know the days of the markets, the flower market in the colonnade or the fruit market, and the timings of the churches. You know, things like that."

"Have you been to the Brancacci chapel... it's considered the Sistine Chapel of the early Renaissance?" enquired Arthur, pursuing conversation.

"Oh yes, the famous fresco cycle. We were able to get in just before closing... Masolino, Masaccio and Filippino Lippi. Some scaffolding obscured one or two of the frescos... restoration in Florence must be constant," Nina said. Fumbling in her pocket she produced a ticket stub, "I kept the ticket... it's a detail of 'The Tribute Money' by Masaccio, the master of solid figures and real space."

Arthur leaned over to see the image and nodded. He was looking at her delicate hands and white fingernails, a little dirty but small and slender, before continuing with pride for his adopted city.

"Florence is very proud of its craftmanship, there are many trained and skilful people in the city helping to restore works of art as faithfully as they can... there'll always be controversy over how to conserve something... but you'll also find the continuation of traditions... methods that have been laid out for hundreds of years... little businesses and trades." Arthur hinted and enlightened, Nina listened attentively. Tuition from books was one way, but knowledge from individuals was much more appealing; the eye and the ear could focus. The tone of his voice was a rich liquid of learning.

"Do you like Ms Barrett's poetry and prose?" she asked him. Staring once again at the large tomb and leaning in carefully to touch the sun-warmed stone, she determined every sense should have its thrill.

"Yes," he replied, "but I'm also interested in her as a person in her own right, her life-story, her love for Robert, her bravery, eloping to Florence... what we know of it anyway. And, well, she's a distant relation of mine… so I dabble in a bit of prose myself… from time to time." He spoke shyly, expressing a little of the Italian by gesturing at his own personal interest.

"A relation… goodness, really?" Nina looked at him as he spoke.

"Yes on my father's side, his mother's maiden name was Barrett and there were many Barrett offspring." She seemed so interested, Arthur felt keen to continue. "During the war… well… my mother took me and my brother back to England to live more permanently. My 'distant' father was a teacher in Kent… we spent some time there together… it was the most time I ever spent with him. He helped me to try and forget the horrors of the war by getting lost in reading and rhyme. *He* used to read me Miss Barrett's poetry. I was only eleven, and didn't really understand but it was all inside a book and that was more amazing than life outside," Arthur nodded to himself. "Best of all, she had a strong connection with Florence, which I missed so much, and then, of course, he told me about our link and where she was buried. At eleven I promised myself, and my father I would visit her and find this green piece of sanctuary, especially after the destruction and chaos of war." Arthur sighed; she was still watching him. "I come so often just to be close… to absorb the air, to have some quiet time away from work and to think. It's not every day the air is of peace and poetry, but it is today."

Nina bent down to smell the Barrett red rose. The warm petals caressed her nose like a scented pillow. *'How I love thee!'* she whispered. How much goodness and beauty has come from visiting this cemetery. Was it rising from the ground or descending from the sky? And although she was alone with Arthur she felt thousands of kindly eyes upon them, willing them to live and to take joy from life; a wonderful pilgrimage they no longer had the opportunity to journey in. A warm shiver ran through her body.

They sat down together on a bench in the shade and as the time passed, they talked.

Nina had thought she was a romantic and had once felt the sarcastic twist of those words, 'you're such a romantic, head in the clouds.' Arthur was a romantic too; she could see it. He always chose the right words and when he spoke you listened to every one of them. He was not economical with his thinking but neither did he indulge in over-long tales. His strong frame and wise eyes were filled with inner complexities, ones he might process and deliver beautifully and openly; ironing out the complications, uncertainties, and intricacies just by being older and more accustomed to the world's ways.

What she could see, and maybe he did too, was they both had a love of art, of learning, of people, of writing, of exploring, of living different lives and seeking out and inspiring the best in others. The latter Nina had had less experience of, but it was clear Arthur was a natural yet gentle leader and a pursuer of talents and heritage.

Perhaps, at first, it was wrong to think so much, but thoughts can move quickly and grow suddenly. It is not always safe to let the mind develop an idea too rapidly; the shock of emotion can be extremely violent, but Nina was already too enthralled. It would not be fair to live so pessimistically, always suspecting that a founded happiness would subsequently lead to a downfall, but neither did she wrap herself up in fairy-tale perfection and perpetual happy endings; real life was not so honest or straightforward. If Nina did not want to live an ordinary life then she shouldn't expect an ordinary route.

Nina and Arthur went back and stood at Elizabeth Barrett Browning's graveside for a while, enjoying the silent breath and hum of the bees and the tender breeze through the undergrowth, shimmering up to the tops of the cypress trees whose tips stirred like the painter's brush, adding a cloud to the blue or erasing one from it. Every living thing seemed in harmony.

Arthur must be mid-fifties thought Nina, and unsurprisingly the most interesting and interested man she had ever stopped to talk to. The sort of man whose every word or sentence might unravel a greater story, or whose conversation could lead to many compelling narratives. Already she thought him a rather singular man. Nina had met boys in their thirties: Tom, Bob, Dan. They were boys not men: kind, sweet, unimaginative and unexciting. Frankly, they were disappointing. Awkward in romance, pedestrian in their thoughts and childish in behaviour, all this was both their fault and a facet of the age. Nina was not willing to wait around for them to grow up. Maybe they were part of a generation package that would not meet her expectations. Her expectations though not exceptionally high, were unusual.

"Shall we move to the gatehouse where there's some drinking water and, well… I'm hot and you must be too… we can sit on one of the stone benches... they're nice and cool," Arthur made the suggestion, stretching out his arm to allow her to see where he meant. Nina didn't want to show reluctance, she thought it a wise idea and she had lingered long enough beside the tomb she had come especially to see. The central pathway, from Ms Barrett's resting place to the gatehouse, would lead her on to a whole new destination.

The bench was a welcome respite. Arthur went to the gardener's hut, miming to the man with a rake for cups of water, who this time noticed Arthur's lady companion looking parched and wearied and a little faint. "Il chiave?" asked Arthur. "È aperto," came the answer. The gardener continued to snip and dead-head flowers, cut-back weeds and comb the tangled grasses. Arthur returned with three waters and gave Nina the one with the most. "It's safe to drink." He sat next to her with absolute ease and confidence as if he had always done so.

"So, where are you and your Aunt Merry staying?"

"The Antica Colonne on the river, it's attached to the Santa Trinita church near the bridge."

"I know it," said Arthur immediately.

Nina assumed it was like telling a Londoner they were staying near Trafalgar Square. Of course, he would know where she meant. He looked like the sort of person who knew everything about everywhere but would have you tell him all the same.

Then for a tense minute she was reminded of her other English self, rushing through an indeterminably long, wet winter with hundreds of other hectic lives; to that rainy, slippery square in London with its windswept fountains, its four imperious lions and the hard thud of the concrete-grey paving stones… and that memory of the waving man. How strange he should come to mind now.

Pulling herself back to the present, Nina asked, "do you work in Florence then… in the three months or are you here at leisure?"

She sipped some of the cold water and felt it trickle down her throat and then strangely chill her toes as if it had skipped all the other organs. Her lungs were filled with a fragrance of freshly raked soil and grassy olive oil, her heart was hot and her pulse was loud in her ear, pounding like the comical beat of a Puccini opera. Nina felt light-headed; she was enjoying finding a new person within, someone original, light-hearted and carefree.

"I'm working in Florence… April, May, June. I… I'd like to show you sometime, I think you might find it interesting… what we do… and it's on a street you won't have found… it's not too far from you either… just over the river… you have to know about it," he said intriguingly.

"I've been down every little street… is it near una piccola bottega di frutta? I found one yesterday, with baskets of vegetables, piles of fruit and a ceiling of hanging salami… and a wall of glass jars with beans and olives and peppers. They had just received an order of Tuscan olive oil from Capezzana. There were cheeses and hams and pastas of every shape… farfalle, pappardelle, rigatoni. The owner was right at the back of the shop and he had to climb over all his boxed orders to reach a packet of pistacchi for me! He really couldn't find anything. It was funny!" Nina realised she had slightly lost Arthur. "Sorry," she said, a bit embarrassed. She was wrong though. He was enchanted and smiled at her enthusiasm *and* he grew more certain of something.

"I think I know the place, Francesco ed Elisabetta's, on… Via dei Federighi… Ha! A wonderful grocer!"

"Do you know the name of all the streets in Florence?" she said teasingly.

"No… well maybe I do… I don't know… my street's rather special. May I come by and collect you tomorrow and show you our little business?"

"Ok, yes… do. I'll see Aunt Merry first and… do you want to meet on the bridge at ten?"

"A good idea… no wait let's meet in front of Santa Trinita church instead, the bridge can get too crowded."

They stayed together in silence for a while, perfectly content. The air was tired of being talked in. It was too hot for birds and the repetitive tapping and snipping of the gardener gave a background percussion to the atmosphere. No-one else entered the cemetery grounds. The traffic had finally calmed and cars were parked and left for the day. Nina took a last glimpse of the English cemetery painting she had stepped into, now she knew what sat between the layers and what extended into the space beyond and quite unexpectedly she would leave feeling uplifted; a strange but true sensation. She felt special and excited and really an invitation to meet a gentleman had not crossed her mind at all. Aunt Merry would see it all religiously and heavenly: as a path of light, the rays spread by goodly angels, the friendly Fates, the hand of destiny and the positive impact of one death on two lives: a circumstance bringing about a situation.

A 'strangeness,' Nina had thought, she was excited by the strangeness. She had left their seat first and not looked around, although she had felt warm eyes upon her back. She was so absorbed in thoughts and conversation past that she did not even think about the sites and architecture on her return route. A feeling more powerful than art was moving her.

Part VI

A Day Out

Arthur reached Santa Trinita half an hour early. The day was once again bright and blue with low, lazy clouds floating artfully in the sky as if to be presented to the viewer for their aesthetic effect. They did not mar the sunshine and its heat, they sailed languidly by to remind the wandering citizen that on high lay the infinite sky, and this sky was far more attractive if fresh, white clouds could be painted upon it.

How odd Arthur felt this morning. He could not remember the last time such confusing and contrasting feelings had engulfed him. He felt boyish and excited, yet uncertain, nervous and fidgety and all these mixed emotions were stirring. They were testing and teasing him and as a result, for long-agitated minutes, he found himself pacing up and down the pavement at the far side of the bridge to stare at the creamy-pink stone of L'Antica Colonne. Only last week he had delivered one of his signature parcels to a client staying in the same hotel and now a stone's throw away, across the river, stayed a woman who had challenged all the senses in him. He undid and re-tied his laces trying to focus. A few conversations raced through his brain, he brushed them off for their silliness and to point out to himself that he was not in fact a teenager but a man of worldliness and good humour and more importantly, as the concept of age-difference between Nina and himself temporarily began to bother him, he could use those many years behind him to great advantage. Yesterday something quite extraordinary had struck him: one young, unusual woman. He was surprised to find such a meeting could trigger emotions he had not come across for as long as he could remember and maybe ones he had not felt before, for he was much older now and his nature well-experienced.

The traffic on the bridge was tight and the pathway narrow. He'd lost count of the number of times he'd crossed this bridge in his life. The same sort of people sitting on the shallow ledges with their luminescent jackets and back-packs; the tour groups gathering with their maps; the cars tooting their horns at over-sized crowds. This backdrop of bridges and the echo of the city's visitors and workers, ready to interact with the artistic offerings of Florence, came to him as new impressions. He felt like a different version of himself, perhaps reinvigorated, and he regarded the world around him as fresh and changed too. Arthur passed the hotel entrance and went to stand in the sun and lean on the soft brown facade of Santa Trinita church. The doorways were shut and he was continuously asked by inquiring, conscientious tourists when the church might be open; clearly, he looked like the sort of gentleman who might know. He managed 'I'm sorry, I don't know,' in three different languages. He was about to be approached by a fourth, a perplexed Japanese family, the father with a permanent crease in his frown, when he stepped out of the vicinity of the holy shadow and walked towards the hotel.

"Hello Arthur," said Nina, beaming a smile with a blush. She was nervous.

"Good morning Nina and how are you... how is your aunt this morning?" He raised his hat and smiled as well. His friendly confidence, which he'd worried had left him or would fail him prior to meeting, returned instantly and as naturally as if it had allowed him his worries but intended to stick by him as all good qualities faithfully do.

"Oh she's a little better... eating a bit more and talking a lot more... all good signs! We haven't dined out for probably five nights... she doesn't feel like trying anything new... it's a shame but she's happy at least."

"Can I help in any way?" asked Arthur, "does she need any medication?"

"No... thank you... I've tried talking to her about going to the pharmacy but she likes to bring her own pills and although she makes a fuss, she doesn't want a fuss." Nina continued, "we talked about the cemetery, she was very inquisitive about the grave and the setting. I didn't tell her I met... well you know...I don't want to worry her...or her temperature." She smiled, slightly apologetically, "so, obviously, she doesn't know I'm out with you today… she's in one of her ask-lots-of-questions but don't listen-to-the-answers kind of mood."

Arthur realised his was not even a name between Nina and her aunt. This didn't bother him. For now, the less known the better; there was a right time for everything.

"Oh… and I've been instructed to bring back a postcard… one of Fra Angelico's frescos at San Marco."

"You haven't been?"

"Oh we did, but ran out of time and I promised I'd buy one when I was out," Nina spoke quickly. She had to get the words out now so she could dispel them, and then leave them behind right where she stood and not think about the intervention of anyone else in her day, not until she had enjoyed her time with Arthur.

"Then we shall… and if that is your aunt's only request… then that is fine with me. Are you ok to go?" Arthur felt bold, his spirit hopeful and he felt strangely liberated and encouraged, not that he had felt tied down or restricted, he just felt elevated and appeared a supremely happy version of his normal self.

"Right, first let's go for coffee… a favourite place of mine… it's not far," Arthur stood roadside next to Nina, he put his hand under her elbow and they walked along several short side-streets, zig-zagging across the cobbled alleys to a long-arched colonnade.

He led her to a corner café called Caffe La Posta with a dark brown canopy, bamboo bushes and open-doors with outside seating. In the doorway stood three polizia smoking cigarettes and sipping espressos in paper-cups. Inside they were grinding coffee beans and squeezing orange juice and there was a mound of sweet and savoury croissants and sugared pastries with wonderful names: cannoli, cannoncini, sflogliatelle. She had been to many cafes before and sampled their delectable treats but somehow, this time, it was more exciting. To be there with Arthur was like walking in with a prince. The polizia and barista staff nodded at him in acknowledgement and he greeted their familiarity in the same way. Maybe he was a prince, or a duke, thought Nina and when he wasn't looking she eyed him suspiciously. He was lovely to look at. Then, realising it was not the time to lapse into such a muse, her eyes fell upon the pastries instead and she lingered on them hungrily, grabbing an extra few seconds to decide, for herself and for him. She had eaten little last night, which had not aroused any concern in Aunt Merry because she too had lost her appetite for complicated dishes and strong flavours. This morning she'd taken tea and dry toast and tried to sound interested in Aunt Merry's plans of a rendezvous with one of the two gentleman guests travelling together. He, Thaddeus, was a vicar at a parish church in The Peak District and apparently the more communicative of the two. Nina had heard neither of them speak, apart from odd pleasantries, but then she had not been inclined to wait around to listen.

They requested three pastries, one of each. With a bit of pointing, Nina attempted to pronounce the tasty names. Arthur ordered the drinks and to make sure she was comfortable, gestured to a table at the fully opened window. The bright morning sunshine had required the unveiling of the café's canopy. Sitting side by side, they looked out towards the high colonnade with its long line of plants and flower stalls. Today, whatever day it was (Nina had lost track, the naming of days did not seem to matter), a vast and various selection of plants were on show. All heights, breadths and fragrances from sweet-green basil pots, raspberry-coloured petunias, yellow-yolk marigolds, sun-worshipping star-daisies to trailing geraniums: something for the kitchen, the balcony and the window boxes. The pretty-petalled bougainvillea were ambitiously climbing up supports, already too short for their tendrils. In a metaphorical fashion Nina thought, when one is happy and cared for, one does grow.

They ate and drank simply, watching the stream of people coming and going like the tide. Nina observed the graceful pace of everyday life as if it were a precious skill and not a rushed affair. She contemplated their moment together and realised that by being with Arthur she saw the world differently. She hoped she had not devoured the

Italian breakfast too quickly. It was flavoursome and messy. Arthur, who'd seen the view from this café as a single man on an ordinary day, felt like a man re-born to all that was there; startled he should have possession of this boyish gaiety. When he considered the droves of people who flocked to Florence, the city of the Renaissance, to discover its culture and beauty, why should he, a near-local, not find a Renaissance of another kind; an encounter and a revelation.

"I've brought a map," Arthur reached into an inner pocket for a small folded map and a pair of glasses, wrapped in a black, slippery, silk handkerchief. He held the soft silk between his fingers for a moment and then rubbed Nina's chin where a crumb was caught. "Just a bit of crumb," he said casually. How embarrassing thought Nina, but it was over in a flash; the softness, the touch, and he quickly averted his eyes.

"We're here… and I'd like to take you… there," Arthur made a cross with his fountain-pen.

"Via… via di fazzo… fazzoletti?" Nina read, "What is fazzoletti… street of something beds?"

"You say it beautifully! Shall we go?" Arthur said pushing back his chair and helping her up.

"Yes please… I'm intrigued… I'm glad the weather's good," said Nina very honestly.

Arthur was unconcerned with the weather, the majority of his time in Florence was spent in perfect temperatures. When it rained it was no matter to him. The skies were not leaden-grey and there was always a universal colour and brightness to the city.

He held out his hand automatically. He had led her here and a hand was the simplest part to touch. Everyday people offered up their hand in greeting. She thought of herself as a writer and how much she relied on her hand to type for work or write in her diary. She had allowed him to take hold of it and it seemed the most natural thing in the world.

It was a little difficult to talk so Arthur and Nina walked in harmony while the sounds of the bustling and flamboyant city echoed around them. They wandered steadily over the Santa Trinita bridge into the Oltrarno district. Stopping at safe intervals to see a new angle of Florence, Arthur highlighted some points of interest, trying not to appear like a guide but a gentle usher. She would want to know and he was keen to tell her. This area was a land of small side-streets made up of architecturally precarious houses with shops of interesting collectables. There was a masks and murals shop, an authentic hat shop, studios specialising in restoration, individual workshops and homely trattorie. Beyond lay the imposing Palazzo Pitti.

Arthur could walk these streets blindfolded. He knew every curve and the style of every shop-front, the design of their stonework and the quaint diversity of each little emporium. He knew the long-established family names and the old, worn and weathered fonts that advertised their wares, and he knew their wooden-framed, scratched-glass windows displaying their business. By now he could even estimate the light-timings of the lampposts, and waited for the daily scents to seep into the air and accentuate the hours of the day: rosemary foccacia, garlic, stew. Every owner and worker was his friend, as loved and respected as relatives might be, united in their principles of trade and tradition. Having lost the grip of Nina's hand, he now took it back, and used his eyes to guide her attention to look upwards at a street sign written in thin, black lettering on a white background: Via di Fazzoletti. It was indeed a street and a street of good company: antique and leather shops mixed with local foodstuffs, their crates of fruit and veg piled in stacks on the pavements. Little groups of men were smoking in patches of sunlight, craftsmen rested their tired limbs and burnished complexions on benches and stools. There was a feeling of energy and vibrancy and creativity as well as exhaustion and fatigue. The Italian maker, whether owner or employee, seemed to work laboriously; tire, feed and rest and then repeat the process, dedicated equally to his work and later to his leisure. The adventurous tourist-buyer mingled with the optimistic Florentine-seller, each in a state of enthusiastic apprehension, one for a good purchase and the other for a good price.

"Yes but, what is a fazzoletti?" asked Nina, knowing this time he would answer.

"I'll show you… follow me, and watch your step… the surface is uneven here," answered Arthur, practically and considerately.

Arthur nodded and gestured to raised heads and eyebrows as he and Nina walked together along the street, stopping in the centre.

"Here we are," Arthur said and he gave Nina time to look at the little shop he had brought her to, "Fazzoletti… diciotto… via di Fazzoletti… Firenze," Arthur whispered warmly in her ear. "Remember that."

"Handkerchiefs?!" cried Nina, looking in the window and then at Arthur enquiringly. He knew he must explain, and he wanted to.

"Yes, that's right… fazzoletti are handkerchiefs," then he added to be clear, "we make them… hand-painted silk handkerchiefs."

The shop-front secured a blind at full stretch to shade the precious articles from a strong and damaging sun. "The sun can be god and devil," mused Arthur, indicating the blind and testing its strength with his long arm. Nina thought she better not repeat this phrase to Aunt Merry. As far as her aunt was concerned the sun was her object of travel and she'd follow it all year if she could. She didn't though, but it was the idea she could if she wanted to that gave her the most satisfaction.

The old, wooden entrance door was off-centre. Either side of it were displayed, very beautifully and elegantly, an assortment of coloured and styled silk handkerchiefs on a velvet background. Nina, having been dazzled by the light, stepped inside the shop and was soothed by the dark interior with its patches of vivid colour. A slight woman with brown, curly hair and glasses, hanging on a cord around her neck, came forward and greeted her with "buongiorno." On seeing Arthur, she flashed a smile and returned to her counter where she finished polishing a dresser and handling some receipts and orders. She grabbed Arthur's momentary glance and diligently handed him some papers, "due messaggi per te," she hushed. Nina saw and heard none of this familiar activity; some moments appear and disappear so quickly they are overlooked and not recorded at all, especially by one so entranced by the beauty around her, yet it's certain they must have happened. It was Arthur, following behind, who became the observer of all before him. Nina relaxed in the cool interior where special lighting accentuated the patterns and pictures on the folded and unfolded handkerchiefs, safe inside display cases, as high as the ceiling, each like miniature works of art. Close behind her stood Arthur, she could sense his warmth and, exhaling a nervous breath, felt she could almost determine the look on his face of happiness and anticipation.

"Gosh, they're beautiful… do you make these?" she said, wanting to compliment and to not sound too amazed.

"This is the oldest shop on the street… there used to be so many craft workshops along here… there's been a handkerchief supplier and producer on *this* site since the sixteenth century…" said Arthur, proudly. "It's my mother's ancestry… the family line is not always straight… you know… like dynasties… peerages and titles… anyway *we've* taken care of it for… oh… thirty years."

"We?" asked Nina, surprised at herself for having picked up that word out of all he was telling her. Who was the 'we' in all this beauty? She waited cautiously for his answer. Nina reflected quickly on the *thirty years,* she wasn't even thirty, just two years off it, and he'd been working for as long as she'd been alive; it didn't need repeating.

"My brother… well, half-brother, but it's not like that… we're as close as brothers might be… mother's son by her second husband… father was… well… he wasn't… that was it… huh! He wasn't always around." Arthur stopped, aware she was listening yet he wished to go no further. The topic was handkerchiefs and his shop, the other personal, complicated stuff could wait, there was time; he would make sure there would be plenty of time. Nina turned back to look at the array of handkerchiefs, this time taking it upon herself to climb a small set of wooden steps which stood directly in front of her, meant for admiring those at a higher level. She even took the nearby magnifying glass to study the patterns and styles as she had once done with a set of charming snuff boxes, but these handkerchiefs were exceptionally intimate. This was Arthur's domain and his heritage.

"Anyway…" continued Arthur, holding the perfectly safe steps she was standing on. He thought it was best to get back on track and into a comfortable, knowledgeable zone, and seeing Nina totally absorbed was very encouraging. The Signora at the counter cocked her head to the side and beamed another knowing smile. She had furtively smiled earlier but neither Nina or Arthur had seen it. On the outside, as the viewer, infatuation and fascination between two people was easy to recognise and that is exactly how the Signora saw these two. She could see there was a connection between them, physically and spiritually. She was quick to make amorous associations; their bodies were close, there was a shine in Arthur's eye, he looked relaxed, upbeat, a more spirited version of himself, all signs of something different, something stirring in him, something he'd found to re-ignite his heart. They were not ordinary friends standing together and Arthur was not paternally attentive, his approach was entirely different, more romantically attached, concerned in sentimental ways. Arthur would have seen this himself if he'd observed his own actions, but because he was clearly a different generation, the ordinary onlooker might have thought it odd. Not an Italian. Perhaps it is true, the Italians are always thinking about love, where to find it or how to express it and how it changes the whole appearance of life, from the day to the night. In general, the English seem stifled and correct, if the Italians feel something as glorious and as beautiful as love, everything in their life shines. They are passionate and expressive and how could they not be with more sunshine to warm their souls and yet Arthur's English side could bring steadiness and propriety.

While Nina eyed the handkerchiefs, Arthur began his commentary. The Signora snuggled herself into a side corner beside the till and focused on her threads and stitches. Signora Liza, as she liked to be called, (for this was not her real name, it was her shop name) a working name of independence, craft and ability. At the workshop she was not a mother, a wife, or a daughter-in-law, here she was Liza, artist and cultivator. Liza was of one of the old Florentine families and no doubt bore some very distant relation to Arthur. Any similarity between them now was merely a case of having worked together for many years, sharing a similar love of silk artistry and the 'blessed' handkerchief. Arthur liked to call them blessed for when people sneezed it was the custom to say 'bless you', perhaps reach for a handkerchief and wish a person good health, 'salute.'

Signora Liza must have heard Arthur's speech a thousand times, except that this time there was a new, intense look about him. He wanted to teach and to interest, not court a sale, but he realised too, that this was a courting of its true meaning. Comfortable in his surroundings, Arthur was fully aware of his attraction to Nina. He had singled her out and longed for more time together. It did not need to be full of talk and discussion, just an affectionate closeness. He reddened at the thought as it came before him and she looked at him suddenly as if he had said her name aloud or she had heard that very thought. Yet this shop, Fazzoletti, was a home to him and space to uphold a family tradition and continue a legacy. The cemetery had also been a safe, quiet and sacred place so really there was nothing odd about the environment; he toyed with these thoughts that flooded his head. It had been such a long time since love had flowed through his mind and soul and taken possession of waking and sleeping and daily living. Now he was twenty-five years older and histories have been made but the feelings, the tingling heat, the new-found openness, the secret excitement – as if each of the six senses had been stroked by a warm hand and voice and had awoken a new person inside.

"Italy was once the most important silk producer of the Medieval age… in Europe that is. In Lucca, not far from here, there was silk production and silk trading as early as the twelfth century… in Florence… we had silk production too. Then, of course, there were the silk routes, over land and sea, connecting the East and the West, allowing cultural trade to be established." Arthur was watching Nina as he spoke. Her ears had given over to his talk but her eyes were fixated on the handkerchiefs, each one a miniature piece of art, which is exactly what they were, painted silk canvases.

"Yes, I'm following… about the silk route?" Nina

turned her head to another handkerchief and sighed, this time she stared at a delicate crimson silk square, with light specks of gold and fine gold stitching. "Something for a Renaissance duchess?" she said, smiling.

"Not that one!" Arthur sounded more serious as he continued, then tried to lighten his voice, "but we know the European traders returned from the far East with headscarves and these were then picked up by the wealthy and used as a fashionable accompaniment to their dress. Mary Queen of Scots held a handkerchief at her execution, as did Charles I, but they don't all have negative connotations. Many were given as christening presents to crowned heads of Europe, Russian Tsars, heirs to thrones and dynasties. In some fifteenth century Renaissance portraits… the ones I studied… women and men held a white embroidered cloth edged in lace… er… in these designs," Arthur said, pointing to a small range, "we've been inspired more by the colours of Renaissance clothing... the richer tones... but here are a few white ones… popular in the wedding season… this month and September too. Just sold two lovely white ones to an American woman… she was staying at your hotel."

"Oh… really… how funny," Nina said, unconcerned, but not rudely so. Days back at the hotel were the issues of someone else's life, as if all those she had met on this trip before Arthur were simply peripheral characters in a play, coming and going and leaving no detectable trace. "I don't think I could part with any one of these," she said ardently, almost too attached to the subject, yet also too involved to care whether she was behaving or saying the right thing. She was with Arthur and he made her different, and this difference was a better version of herself.

"They're lovely... so fine and delicate... you could never use them..." she let her sentence trail off. Not one of these handkerchiefs was to be used in the practical sense. They were to be admired. A handkerchief's original function might be fine for cotton, but not for these exquisite silks.

"Well... I'm glad you like them." Arthur took a step back from the small ladder to gaze at Nina. To ensure there was no long, awkward silence or that he might be caught by her perceptive eye, he continued his narration, although he had forgotten the Signora's presence. Liza was a sculpture in form but her mind was racing with acute and tender observations and her lips curved into a gentle smile as she watched Arthur. He could not be more than ten years younger than her, for he seemed, in all manners, to have dropped years off his roving life.

"We rely hugely on the tourist trade now, our business is mostly word of mouth... like every one of the shops on this street... and footfall is quite good along here... between the Santa Trinita bridge and the Ponte Vecchio, sandwiched between the Pitti Palace on one side and Santo Spirito on the other, certainly less touristy than the riverside shops... full of charm, quite unchanged from the days of the Grand Tour." Arthur swallowed several times to moisten his drying throat. "The handkerchief is an unusual gift…not cheap mind… but extremely adaptable… for travel… you know… it's light and soft… and unique… something Florence offers that's different from other European cities." Arthur stopped abruptly, he could have gone on and on with a little more history and his well-conceived sales pitch. It was honest and persuasive, simple without being pushy and dominant. It did seem to add to her enjoyment. They had lost customers once, just by hiring the wrong sales assistant; it had been his brother's idea and it was a lesson well-learnt.

Signora Liza was proud of Arthur in a maternal way. The boys had done well to keep the tradition alive and to save the shop from the hardships many small businesses had faced. Harsh financial periods had been a problem. Cheap imports, fakes and clever copies had debased their efforts and prestige. Signora Liza was particularly good with the French, German and Spanish clients while Arthur handled the British, Americans and occasional Australian clients as did his brother when he took over Arthur's shift. His brother tended the summer and autumn period. Did he need to explain this to Nina? Maybe, just casually.

"So, I'm here at the shop for my three months… April, May, June then Simon… my said brother takes over. We're closed to the public in the winter months."

With more ties at home than his brother, a three-month period was more suited to Arthur's lifestyle.

Arthur helped Nina off the small ladder, knowing she really did not need the assistance, in fact he got in the way and caused her to trip. There was not much space inside the shop, groups were asked to come in four at a time. There were no opening times on the door, the only sign read: no backpacks/ senza zaini. Arthur did not like a cramped shop and was willing to turn certain types of people away if necessary. He refused a man entry with his dog, a woman pushing a double pram and just then a student with a rolling suitcase, twice his width.

"Oh sorry!" Arthur said, annoyed with himself and feeling the clumsy side of his attractive height. The slip meant he could touch her shoulder and he looked about for a chair. Signora Liza cleared her throat and finished with a light cough, signalling her position in the dark corner, thinking it was time she reminded them of her presence despite rather enjoying the delightful floorshow of a way into love.

"Il fazzoletto… it was a symbol of many things… lurve, 'ope… come si dice gioia?" Signora Liza spoke, then realised her English was not as clear as she had thought.

"Joy," said Arthur.

"Si, gioia… loss, sadness, moda… er… celebrazione, commemorazione, anniversari." She knew Nina, who was watching Liza's mouth move up and down, was smart enough to follow her gist. Both ladies' eyes fell upon Arthur, Nina's in a look of admiration and Liza's in a look of affection, she was Italian after all. Liza had once told Arthur that Italians take time in life to do things because all their words are longer and more flowery to pronounce, once their work is accomplished, their lives are lived and loved to the full; at least she meant something along these lines. A generalisation on the mentality of any race would often be done by the tourist but Arthur was a mixture of two cultures, favouring the openness of the Italians and the steadfastness of the British. What was she, Liza, saying at this moment with her dark pupils and hazelnut-coloured eyes? Some ancient Latin motto inscribed on a family crest: True love is a reward to be nurtured and not a prize to be won.

"It's true the handkerchief was... is still... an item of fashion... these are quite luxurious... we have simpler styles too... here." Arthur opened a long, polished wooden drawer with two brass handles, lined once again in velvet, where more silk handkerchiefs lay, neatly overlapping one another. They were much plainer and in three sizes, not one alike.

"Each one is unique," he had made that clear. "We want our products to reach all pockets. Ha!" said Arthur, realising his joke before moving on, "the handkerchief has been adapted throughout history... and in some cases defined it... like the war, for instance. When bombing missions were carried out the pilots used a handkerchief to sketch out the area of countryside... if they were shot down... they had an escape map. And then the Depression... when ladies would have to forgo a nice new dress or new hat... a handkerchief... cotton of course, was less costly... it could liven up or change their outfit... highlight a colour in a top pocket... however they liked. They were... resourceful and imaginative, I suppose."

"How clever," said Nina, fascinated. She didn't want Arthur to see her worried frown; the matter of *that* handkerchief was preying on her mind. On entering Arthur's shop, she had thought of the one she owned, the one from the rainy, February afternoon at the post-office in London, delivered into her hands by an unexpected, dignified saviour. She had thought of the man, but he existed as a vision, no more, for Arthur was real and breathing and standing beside her.

How and when should she tell Arthur about it? It was a vivid red, rose-painted silk handkerchief she cherished and had slipped into the inner sleeve of her suitcase. It was similar, and as beautiful as the touching pieces displayed in his shop. It must be of the same quality, value and of equal distinction. She had looked over her handkerchief again and again. How crude it would be to just blurt out, 'I've got one,' and then argue over its authenticity. Thankfully it was Signora's feisty accent and funny English that diverted Nina's thinking.

"Arturo say to Nina... 'bout il movimento Libero e di Pira!" she said proudly, encouraging Arthur to tell the tale she liked best to hear.

"Very well, I will." Arthur closed the shop door and pulled down a blind, something he now wished he'd done earlier. Signora Liza remained still, once again a statue.

"In the second world war, we... not me personally... but the company... designed a special handkerchief for the free Italians... those... well, an underground faction, secretly fighting against Mussolini's Fascist regime and his alliance with Hitler. The free-men, as they were known, had connections throughout Europe, but it was very dangerous... extremely dangerous. Any civilians found participating in the Resistance were executed. Then... when Mussolini was deposed in 1943, the Italian leaders withdrew from their German alliance and signed an armistice with the Allies. But the Germans overran Italy's cities, causing tremendous devastation and death." Arthur continued, always entranced by this story, his story, his history; it still moved him as if it were the first time spoken. "Our handkerchief... soft to touch... fragile... hidden away... was a language and a gesture and a silent vocabulary, that... I am so thankful to say... was never discovered by the enemy. While they were intercepting papers, deciphering codes, destroying, persecuting and looting, the object of our handkerchief was overlooked. It was a handkerchief, simple as that, but it was a symbol of an extremely important cause... like a signal of revolt… of brotherhood. They were used like paper with notes and ciphers… and became the badge of fraternity… of a guild, certainly something Italians would have understood having had guilds for hundreds of years… a great upholder of strength, resilience and belief in desperate times.'

Nina was riveted by Arthur's story and although Signora Liza knew little of the English he was saying, she knew all of the tale he was telling. Her eyes looked weak and watery. She was hot with reflective pain and anger; a part of the past that would not leave her memory. She was too young to remember the suffering but it was in her family's blood, and would remain in her.

"E Pira, Pira!" exclaimed Liza. She seemed anxious this name had not been mentioned. She had deliberately encouraged the tale and Arthur had stopped talking; it would be incomplete without Pira. Life in Italy must always be filled with conversation. Someone must be chattering, preferably several people should be talking over one another and a variety of conversations should be flowing in unison. Any topic might be discussed, from the most trivial to the most important, it did not matter. Everything was given air-time and therefore it was given an opinion, whether it was with grunts or long-heated arguments, very little was forgotten. The Italians had a long history and a long memory.

"Yes… yes… then there was Pira… Giorgio La Pira, a celebrated figure to the Florentines… a demonstrative and outspoken man… he built a strong anti-Fascist campaign throughout Florence… but he had to flee… to Siena first and then on to Rome, where he was protected." Arthur drew a thoughtful breath and Liza leant forward on the edge of her seat. "Well… I'm… *we're* proud to say he, Pira, had one of our handkerchiefs." Arthur turned to Liza and she nodded her head vigorously. "He was very active during the war years, speaking forcefully against the Fascists and when Mussolini finally fell…" Arthur paused, "Pira continued to show his love for Florence… he became mayor of the city… when the war ended… and helped to rebuild it." Arthur sighed, looked about his shop and to Nina who stayed silent.

"Oh… he reconstructed the poor, devastated city… building neighbourhoods with gardens… local shops… a sense of community that still survives today… markets, schools, churches, green spaces. He really thought about what people needed… what was important to them… by restoring the desolate areas he was restoring lives as well… and he created jobs… and self-esteem… and hope. All these things he stood for."

"And all this time he had one of your freedom handkerchiefs?" asked Nina.

"Yes… he did! Oh, and with his effort many of the bridges were rebuilt too… like the Santa Trinita… the one…"

"The one we walked over today… that I see from my window?" added Nina.

"Er… yes that's right."

"What did it look like… your freedom handkerchief? Is there one here?" Nina asked keenly.

"Well we've always favoured dark green in many of the designs… like the green of an Italian olive oil or the hillsides… so it had a thick, dark-green edge… of course it really had to be dark, camouflaged… as simple as possible… we didn't want to attract the wrong attention with a bright red pattern or a stark white. If the Fascists had known what it represented it would have been fatal. Pira was exceptionally forthright, but mostly people kept their ideas secret and carried on as 'free-Italians' in fear. Families could be torn apart by different ideologies." Arthur moved over to the counter to lean on its solid support, keeping his eyes directly on Nina. She was so interested in him; it was if she might be drawing the story from the depth of his soul.

He continued pensively, "so back to your question… a thick, dark-green edge… dark-blue in the centre, with dark blue stitching around the outside, on the green. It was quite small, easy to slip into a pocket or tuck away safely. Smaller than the ones we make today. Then… on the bottom right-side, stitched in black were the letters I… L… both in capital letters.'

"I… L," repeated Nina.

"Italia Liberta!" cried Signora Liza, louder than she had intended.

Arthur looked at Nina and smiled softly; she could feel a tear forming at the corner of her eye. Liza snuggled back into her chair, polished the edge of the counter with her cardigan sleeve and pushed over a notepad and pen so that Arthur might show Nina just how the design looked. He took the pen. He's left-handed thought Nina and slanted her head to watch him draw.

"I and L spell il… which is 'the' in Italian so the pairing of the two letters is not unusual… I think it was a good choice… and I guess it worked. When word spread what it meant to own one of these handkerchiefs… we issued a great many and they got around. We agreed a donation would suffice… no one should have to pay for freedom… all they had to do was be careful. We heard later some stories from families across Italy that by owning one of our handkerchiefs… they were holding on to freedom… clasped to a belief and… the hope of making it through the worst days of their lives."

"The only person I know who has one is Liza," said Arthur, looking at Signora rooted to her chair.

She nodded her head once again, as enthusiastically as before. How this dear Italian woman could be so robust, happy and positive while the tears of emotion rolled down her cheeks was a sight to see, and with all the handkerchiefs around her, she found a plain box of tissues, dabbed her eyes and wiped her face.

"Si, si," she sniffed, "ne ho uno."

"Yes... Liza has one... but it never leaves her house... wrapped in tissue in a shoebox... it was her father's and will one day be her son's." Arthur reached out his hand and rubbed Liza's left shoulder tenderly. "It's rare we get through a day without a few tears from Liza... but I admit this is a hard... and wonderful story to celebrate."

"I don't know what to say," said Nina, feeling foolish for uttering such a boring set of words, but thinking if she said nothing it could add nothing of value.

"I suppose there are some, or many, I don't know a number... dotted about the country... overseas. The movement of people and migration... it's uncertain where one will turn up. After the war many people stayed very quiet about their war experiences... trust and faith and friendships had been broken and recuperation took a long time... as for healing, that takes longer."

Arthur was tiring now and felt touched by his own words. Perhaps he was making Nina uncomfortable. "People didn't want to look back, they wanted a future. No doubt our handkerchiefs got put away, lost, forgotten. Like I said, some heart-warming stories crop up from time to time... but if the war generation didn't share their stories, they were lost too... and the symbolism of our handkerchief goes with it.'

By the time Arthur checked his watch it was mid-afternoon. Signora Liza had disappeared, only to reappear with a packed lunch; she didn't like to leave her counter-side. He felt they had been in the shop too long, in a time capsule. He felt pressured, almost trapped by his own web of words. Now he wanted to open the door onto the 20th century and breath its air into his lungs, that it might make him youthful again; it certainly made him appreciate his place in time.

"Are you hungry Nina… shall we get a bite to eat?" asked Arthur, perhaps with some nourishment he might feel released, from the shop, from responsibility. He loved the place yet worried about its position into today's world. The burden of its future lay with him and Simon, and after that who would take care of the next stage of its faint working life? 'We're the last handkerchief shop left on via di Fazzoletti' he had told Nina and he didn't want his generation to fail the next.

Nina did not feel like anything to eat but she said yes just the same. She could see Arthur was pale and she wanted to be with him, though she would not question him any further over handkerchiefs and dynasties and the war. They wandered out into the dusty street where the warm afternoon sun bathed their faces. Arthur took hold of Nina's hand. In two days, a change had come over him and it felt good, no, it felt wonderful. He was holding this woman's hand, a warm gesture he had missed. It made him a better person, quite a different person from what he had been before, something akin to love or maybe it wasn't akin, maybe it was love and the more he reflected, as he walked Nina further into local Florence, the happier and hungrier he became.

Part VII

Two days on

Aunt Merry was conscious she was not the best companion for Nina. It was not simply a matter of age and interests; she had been unwell and it was a very inconvenient thing. Nina had reassured her aunt that she was quite happy. With a good week left, she was content to live in the city as locals do and take pleasure in the little touches of individuality that she had walked so briskly past before, on her way to other destinations. In short, she was learning to slow down and 'look up with care' as her aunt had always suggested.

In this brief span of time Aunt Merry had managed to strike up a good relationship with the vicar, Thaddeus. His companion, whose name she had not caught, despite asking twice, was as quiet as a mouse, possibly even mute for no-one would choose to visit a vibrant, holy city such as Florence and live within its walls so silently. Then again, she had considered the spiritless disposition of the lowly Serge and thought, 'wonders will never cease.' Thinking momentarily on the shadow of Serge, she realised she had not seen 'a whisker of him for days' and wondered with half a care whether he had left the hotel completely. It was such a fleeting thought that by the time she came around to discussing her main objective with Nina, it had sunk to the bottom of her mind like a pebble in a pond. Aunt Merry was modern in many ways and archaic in others, you could never quite tell which way she might lean on any given topic. She seemed greatly in favour of diversity amongst people and yet she also wondered (you could tell from her facial expressions; a family trait affecting the females) why people were not - fundamentally - more like herself; a personality in which she took great pride and enjoyment.

"Thaddeus and his friend... er... his friend... I forget his name... anyway they've decided to hire a car and have very kindly invited me... Oh! and I'm sure they'd be very happy to take you as well... to join them... us. We're going to visit some of the churches in the hilltop towns near here and it's a great chance to see the surrounding countryside of Tuscany... but we do want to see the churches." Aunt Merry spoke sweetly to Nina, at first almost encouraging her to come along and join their cosy party and then adding little details that might discourage her too. "The journey might be very bumpy... the roads are not good... in some parts the roads are very windy and they suffer terribly from pot-holes... Italians won't fix them. Thaddeus promised me a front-seat... you know how queasy I can get... especially after this nasty patch I've been through." Aunt Merry did a little dry cough to conjure an effect. She was actor, writer and director of her own little scene and essentially, she knew it would work. Nina need find no excuse for declining, it seemed Aunt Merry had given her the answers and when Nina sighed relief, she worried her aunt had detected disappointment.

"I think I'll stay put... there are some shops I want to look in..."

"Very well I thought you'd feel that way... no bother whatsoever... as long as you're happy doing what you want... that's fine." Aunt Merry was glad to have a new adventure in place, and Nina saw freedom and peace of mind for the next few days. She could not stop thinking about Arthur.

The previous night she had gone to bed with visions of him in her head; standing in his shop surrounded by handkerchiefs and the tales he was reciting being acted out as he conjured them up. In the morning she tried to eat a small pastry while Aunt Merry filled the toasted air with talk on the large amount of dust clinging carelessly over many of the museum sculptures. Iconic statues she had had the infinite joy of witnessing for the first time and yet failed to understand why no-one was paying attention to their fabric. 'They need to take better care of their heritage,' she had bemoaned and with comments such as this Nina found her aunt, without seeming to realise it herself, was rapidly returning to her heady state of normality with every sip of tea.

Nina and Arthur had agreed to meet two days after the shop visit. Arthur was expecting a good turn of business just before the weekend and wanted to be on hand to deal with enquiries and sales. Of course, Nina had thought, this was the reason for his time in Florence, she had forgotten about work and commitment and had lost any sense of time. She was away on holiday, he was not; it was an ordinary week for him. For Arthur, there was nothing ordinary about this May week; his life was undeniably altered. Oddly, the thrill of such feelings worried him slightly, but he was thankful and inspired, scribbling poetical lines on safe scraps of paper usually reserved for new handkerchief sketches. In line with the seasons, Arthur normally designed four new patterns a year and now found he had conceived five separate ideas.

On seeing Nina and the little talking they had done, it was as if the world had opened up new rooms for him to enter, yet at the same time he was acutely aware of the brevity of life. All he wanted to do was embrace the era he was peacefully living in - no wars, no conflicts – and be faithful to his ambition of leaving a legacy. It was difficult to describe exactly why this young woman Nina had stirred his mood. She had depth which was a refreshing change from the many shallow women he had met; women who were forgettable, one indistinguishable from the next. With Nina it was entirely different, something kept her very strong and upright, self-assured and assertive; a woman with whom you could talk of anything. Maybe he had known her before, in another time, he did not dwell on it; the past had been written, the future was waiting to be filled. With these thoughts racing through his head, he climbed on his green motorbike, sparkling in the sunshine and headed for Nina's hotel. He was ten minutes late, he could not explain why.

Arthur, dressed in dark leather, came to an easy stop and perched the bike on the kerb next to Nina. He handed her a helmet and helped secure the band while she held her sunglasses in place.

"Hello… and good morning!" said Arthur.

"Morning… another lovely day!" said Nina looking up at the sky, with a heavy head of helmet.

"Come let's go… there's a place in Fiesole with a wonderful view of all Florence… it's about…"

"Villa San Michele?" asked Nina. She wanted to sound as if she too was well-acquainted with the popular weekend destinations of a Florentine.

"Ha! No, my dear I shan't take you there… that's where all the tourists go…" he said pointing up at the hotel, indicating it was the haunt of the rich visitor to be sent to Villa San Michele. "That's the last place I'd take you."

She knew he meant well but the lines seemed awkward, a bit terse and clipped. Only two days had passed since being together and already it felt like a week and the gap needed fixing; a bit of the glue that bonded them had come loose. It would take time to re-adjust to each other's ways and company. She felt, with a combination of her sprightliness and his tone and turn of phrase, a bit childish. Perhaps he was nervous, she detected a little edginess; it was rather mis-placed she thought.

"There's another villa up on the hillside... Villa Angelo... no weddings... no functions... it's much quieter and..." said Arthur leaning in, conscious her ears were a little hidden under the helmet. "And... I think you'd like it best... yes... I'd like it better if you were there with me. Let's see what you think... now hold on to my belt... I'll ride... I mean I do ride very safely... don't worry."
"I'm not worried... let's go then," said Nina, smiling, her confidence returning.

Once out of the centre of the city the roads up to Fiesole were twisting and winding. Nina held on tightly to Arthur's belt with her right hand and found she was naturally hugging him with her left arm, whilst moving her head back and forth, admiring the greenery on either side of the road on this slow, convoluted journey. They were rising upwards, further and further away from the dusty pinks of Florence to a fresh, sun-warmed landscape where the air was cool and as grassy and peppery as a Tuscan olive oil. She could taste it on her tongue and inhaled it through her nose, it seemed to flavour everything, most of all it was the very moment she was savouring.

Villa Angelo was a soft, sandstone-coloured villa, modest in size, elegantly proportioned and perfectly classical. At the top, in the very centre, was a triangular pediment spreading the width of three of the five ground-floor arches. Below was the first floor about two-thirds the height of the ground; two open windows interspersed by three lion heads. At ground level rounded arches with pilasters, also mirrored on a smaller scale above, formed a warm, sleepy portico filled with flowering urns and hanging lamps. The main entrance was through the third archway. A grand, ancient, carved wooden door lay open; the dark interior seemed appealing after the bright sunshine. They had parked on a white gravel patch, marked 'le moto.' It was surrounded by four neat, low-cut, box-hedged gardens, with ornamental olive trees and white geraniums. Arthur and Nina took a moment to gather themselves: hair, clothes and a bag of Nina's she'd clung to more tightly than she'd thought. Arthur took both their helmets and placed them next to the bike then reached for her hand and walked confidently across the drive. They did not pass through the middle archway and into the inviting cool and mysterious dark but wandered round to the side of the villa.

"Look," Arthur said, nodding his head upfront. He'd underestimated her curiosity and quick-wittedness. He could tell she was perceptive and smart for already she'd gasped at the beautiful sight that lay before them. Her eyes stung, trying to fit the scape into a full and clear vision. There, in a hot and early summer haze, lay the entire city of Florence surrounded by a green belt of rolling wild country and the sfumato blue hills of a Leonardo da Vinci painting.

"How… glorious," better words seem to fail Nina. The picture spoke for itself as they walked slowly under the loggia at the side of the villa, every archway filled by a view of the city. The famous Brunelleschi Duomo sat splendid at the centre, defining Florence. Not one piece of surrounding architecture could reach higher or dared obscure its vaulted majesty. The dome bestowed a focal point: it endowed a completeness in its ability to both diffuse and mirror the discreet yet unique dignity of Florence.

The ceiling of the loggia was frescoed. The paint, reds, greens and ochre, had faded; they were slightly cracked and worn, aged and delicate. Nina had to crane her neck; she stopped to gaze at the faces staring down. How many people must these holy saints have witnessed passing through this passage, admiring the scenery and wondering at the vastness and richness laid bare. The flower pots and urns were this time planted with red geraniums and white hydrangeas. Arthur took Nina's hand which had slipped from his grasp when she had lingered under one of the archways. He led her into the broad, stepped garden, set with white parasols and white-cushioned furniture. It looked like the most comfortable dream: great, wide sun-drenched umbrellas protecting cosy deep-filled chairs. The white colour seemed to indicate luxury and purity and heavenly space; a soft seat on which to rest your body and grow your dreams. Arthur sat down and Nina joined him. There was no-one else there: no eyes, no glare. If you required attention, it seemed the service would find you and as soon as they did, menus and glasses of bottled water from a nearby source were efficiently placed on the glass side-table. It did feel like a dream, quiet and as ideal in form as dreams can be, but a warm breeze, gentle sighs and the humming of bees made it expand into the dimension of reality. How truly wonderful, thought Nina. She could feel very comfortable in expensive settings but she did not expect it or take anything for granted. She appreciated the lavish hospitality of her aunt just as she recognised the trouble to which Arthur had gone.

Arthur ordered two coffees and some sandwiches. Nina admired the terracotta tubs of lemon trees, heavy with their bright yellow fruit, as large as grapefruit with a daisy-style blossom that smelt of pierced citrus zest.

"So… what do you think?"

"What do I think?" she repeated, like an introduction to her following statement, "I think it's the most beautiful place I've ever seen." Nina had thought about the view from the terrace at the hotel Antica Colonne, which only a week or so ago she had thought the most incredible sight, and so it was no doubt, but this surpassed all. She knew this because it gave her a shiver down her spine; a slight tingle of excitement ran through her veins and propelled her spirit into adventure and the wonderful thing about adventure, it was unchartered territory and unexplored emotions. It was not often that one single view could have such an affect. She was there with Arthur and his presence was not to be underestimated.

"I hoped you'd say that!" said Arthur, "I apologise if I'm a bit agitated... I haven't been here for a long time."

"How long?"

"Five maybe six years..." he said, looking at her, uncertain; such a period of time meant nothing in the history of Florence. "The Villa's been in the same family for generations. It's a hotel now. You can always spot a member of the family... they've all inherited the prominent 'Angelo' nose... it's more pronounced in profile."

"Do the family know you?"

"Someone might recognise me... from the past... from Florence. We'd just nod a hello or maybe shake hands... anyone who comes to Villa Angelo is usually looking for some time to be alone and... to be invisible... unless, of course they've actually come to do business."

"I see," said Nina. She didn't need to delve too deeply into what 'business' meant in Italian terms.

"Anyway, my point is..." said Arthur, keen to get to an important story he found sometimes difficult to put into words, because he rarely did so. It was a tale now running around his mind but not on his tongue.

"My uncle… my maternal uncle, Piero, brought me here as a boy… when I was… well I had to be six, just before the outbreak of the war in thirty-nine. He did a little business everywhere he went but to come here was a real refuge for him… to look down on his precious city. He was always trying to protect it…"

"From the Germans?"

"Yes, definitely… when they came… but before that… Mussolini's dictatorship and his secret police meant free-thinking Italians always had to be careful. They lived most of their lives in fear… anything ever done was always done in secret. Faith was strong but trust… trust… 'fiducia' he used to say it was… *'la cosa più difficile.'*" Nina's lost look prompted Arthur, 'the hardest thing… very rarely he spoke English… it was working in the Fazzoletti shop made him very patriotic."

"He must have been very brave."

"Yes… and very scared."

"Was he a friend of La Pira's?" Nina was conscious she was asking many questions; it was purely because she was interested and it seemed to encourage Arthur too.

Arthur looked a little taken aback. She had every

right to ask, he'd spoken about La Pira's work just as he had about the freedom handkerchiefs.

"We… Simon and I… were schooled in England but always visited Florence with our mother in the holidays. Uncle Piero never left Italy, he maintained the little Fazzoletti shop even when his nerves were fractured… before and after the war. I don't think he knew any other way to live but constantly on edge… but here he was happy… here he was," Arthur paused and looked about in agreement, "most like himself."

"And how was that?"

"Funny… strong… dedicated." Arthur said decidedly and then he leaned in and spoke in a soft voice, 'fear and uncertainty can really drain the colour from a man's pupils and the blood from his face until he looks guilty of some… some contrived charge. Villa Angelo was like a sanctuary to him, a place that gave him distance… perspective on Florence… perspective on life. He prayed here in the private chapel… for strength… for hope. Well… as I grew up and thought about what he'd lived through… well, maybe some of these thoughts and feelings are mine and I attribute them to him. No-one opened up… even now many of the older Italians are unwilling to talk of the war. He was very reserved… even with us… that's why he worked well with the handkerchiefs… symbols rather than words."

A coffee pot, two small porcelain cups, a small jug of cream, a sugar dish and eight finely sliced finger sandwiches arrived on a silver tray. The waiter had appeared like a ghost, very thin, almost invisible. Nina couldn't help but stare at his nose. He managed the weight and contents of the tray with great dexterity. Within a blink the table was arranged and he was gone, so that peace might now mingle with pleasure. The coffee was rich and the sandwiches tasted fresh with light fillings that blended to the taste of the aromatic coffee. It revived them both and prompted Nina to ask more about Uncle Piero. The tale Arthur had intended to tell would be more coherent after three small cups of coffee with two large brown, lava-looking sugar lumps.

"Uncle Piero… sorry it's just I've not spoken about him in a while. *He* was the one who designed the freedom handkerchief… and his extraordinary… historic mission was one that my mother recounted. She did not hear it from Piero… he wouldn't speak to anyone about his assignments… he remained secretive all his life… it was from a relation of Liza's that the majority of the story came to be told… and since then, more war-time stories connected to the freedom handkerchiefs, have reached us." At this point Arthur produced his reading-glasses and polished them with his plain, dark-green handkerchief; it was for no other reason than to concentrate on something simple and close before taking the last sip of cool coffee and a long look at Nina's clear, trusting face.

"It was months after Italy had signed the armistice with the allies... that was in September 1943. Mussolini was no longer in power or allied to Germany, which meant Italy was liable to German attacks and invasion... and they began." Nina, in the heat of the shade, felt the sensation of an ice-cube slide down her back and prepared herself for a fascinating story which she promised not to interrupt with questions.

"In February 1944 Uncle Piero was on an errand to deliver a number of our freedom-handkerchiefs to a place called Monte Cassino. Do you know it?"

"No, I don't."

"It's an ancient, rocky hilltop town... south-east of Rome... and a strategic point on Highway six... the road that leads uninterrupted to Rome. The Germans built a defence line called The Gustav line... it ran from the Tyrrhenian Sea to the Adriatic, from one side of Italy to the other and through the town of Monte Cassino. This line consequently slowed an allied advance for months." Arthur took a few of the remaining sugar lumps; one white represented Monte Cassino, one brown located Rome and two smaller pieces represented the seas. It was an attempt to help illustrate his train of thought.

"Uncle Piero liked to hide the handkerchiefs in the inner lining of a long, warm woollen coat... acceptable in winter. He showed me once... when it was all a game to me. In the summer he found other methods of concealment... but this was February. It was unwise to travel with bags... it raised suspicion... cases or parcels or anything might be inspected, searched or burnt. But everyone felt guilty... you were *made* to feel guilty."

"The freedom handkerchiefs were a symbol of solidarity, of hope... of triumph over adversity... in these painful... fearful years. They were also art... when Italy's artworks were being looted. In a country where art defined its history but had suffered the brutalist architecture of the Mussolini years of dictatorship, my uncle was inspired to give pre-eminence to something small and creative, making a gesture both precious and enormously important. I suppose they were like icons but their religion was freedom. They were transported by the very brave... some were too scared to own one, though many people wanted to be part of free Italy." Arthur's voice sounded very full.

Nina gave him a moment, then pressed him to further disclosures. Arthur seemed nervous... but Nina persevered... "of course so many people risked so much during the terrible war years. Did your uncle just take handkerchiefs? Surely there was more to it than that."

Arthur hesitated, "Liza is the only other person I have told this to and yet still I am indecisive."

Nina watched Arthur's face as he struggled with

his conscience. Finally, he sighed a deep, heartfelt expression of his need to share with this woman the deepest secret of his family.

"I told you that Piero had designed the freedom handkerchiefs. He designed them yes, and they were made in the workshop. At the end of the day when all was dark he would go down to the studio in the shop and check each one individually. What he did was to encode each handkerchief in painstaking detail, almost invisible to the naked eye, working with complex ciphers received from the advancing allied forces to be transported via the Italian underground to the resistance fighters further up the line."

"Did he get there, your uncle?"

"By the time he'd arrived in Monte Cassino the Benedictine monastery had been bombed."

"The Germans?"

"No… it wasn't the Germans, it was the allies… the Americans."

"The Americans… why them?"

"Sadly the British and Indian ground troops were given false information… it was *assumed* the Germans were occupying the monastery as an observational point… but… and I'm sorry to say… it was full of Italian civilians… those who had fled the town nestled below ran to the monastery for safety… two hundred and thirty or more… dead… and much of the town took a hit."

"How terrible."

"Yes, terrible … and ironically… after the bombing the Germans used the monastery ruins as perfect defensive cover."

Nina asked slowly and sympathetically, "and what about your uncle and the handkerchiefs?"

"Uncle Piero stayed for a short while… the war raged on and the people scattered… journeying aimlessly and wildly over the mountains… the monks too, disappeared."

"Did he get through with the coded handkerchiefs?"

"You know, he'd only taken about twenty… it didn't matter how small the number… it was the objective that was the incentive… what each handkerchief represented and how one handkerchief could unite the strength and advancement of so many Italians." Arthur said slightly shakily, "I think… I might have been the same way, but the task of such dangerous ways fell to Uncle Piero. He took it up… like a calling. Mother believed it was just that… she read it once in his eyes, two days before the colour seeped out of them and he went very dark and impenetrable. You can read a lot from a person's eyes… Uncle Piero didn't want to be read…"

"A calling, you said… like a divine intervention?" said Nina.

"Yes… you're right a divine intervention… of sorts," Arthur smiled at the way Nina had termed it. He liked the phrase; he'd think of it this way.

"They had a name you know… they couldn't be called freedom handkerchiefs despite the IL, which was a code of sorts. If you received a handkerchief with IL painted on, you knew there was a cipher contained in the design. To avoid the danger of discovery the common name used for the handkerchiefs was the Holy Trinity handkerchiefs, *I fazzoletti della Santa Trinita.*"

"It was thought they were known as the Holy Trinity because each was folded into three but actually the handkerchief itself represented three important things; the symbol of hope, the making of art, and the transfer of a secret code."

"I don't know about the fate of these handkerchiefs… you never asked him if they were delivered… I assume so… the immediate past was not a place to linger." Arthur paused, "once the handkerchiefs were exchanged, they were never mentioned again and there certainly wasn't any correspondence."

Arthur sat back on his deep, white chair, shut his eyes and put his face to the sun. He needed to gain energy and power some better memories. The sun, always willing to give of itself, beamed its heat on his chilling story. There was a gap of few minutes before Nina spoke.

"But what about after the war?"

"Erm... after the war Uncle Piero worked alongside La Pira... mending morale and helping the Florentine people... but he played no great part in its actual reconstruction. Despite his silent ways he was remarkably good with real people, he understood them... without lots of words... I think La Pira could see his sensitivity, his effect on people. Everyone had to learn how to live again as a result of the war, and how to live in this new peacetime. Many ordinary people, citizens of the country, still feared speaking and expression... although they did support voices like La Pira. Why this must have been the quietest period in all of Italy!" Arthur smiled furtively, trying to add a little humour to his story, but Nina remained quite serious and concerned.

"Uncle Piero did one of the best things a quiet man could do and that was to focus on continuing his trade... making and designing new handkerchiefs. The Fazzoletti shop helped nurture his spirit and gave vitality I suppose, to the local area. Stocks were low and supplies had been difficult but they all managed because... well they had to... what else was there to do, after having been swept so low, now was the time to come back again from despair... from hunger. La Pira even gave Uncle Piero the stamp of the lily... although it *was* given with great discretion. On the surface it appeared as if it had been issued to uncle for his services to the city… but secretly, those few that did know of uncle's war work would associate the stamp with his freedom-handkerchiefs."

"The stamp of the Lily?"

"Si, il timbro di giglio di Firenze…" said Arthur, "it's a red lily on a white background… it's the symbol of Florence. The stamp of the lily is actually a small brooch made by the goldsmiths on the Ponte Vecchio and given to citizens of a distinguished nature… of exceptional bravery, courage and fearlessness… in the face of danger. To come through a war, to keep your nerve and to unite in the name of free Italy; so many men and women were worthy of the stamp… it just belonged to Florentines." Arthur moistened his throat, "he always pinned his brooch on the inside of his jacket, where he also kept a handkerchief. Uncle Piero never became accustomed to wearing any significant item on the outside of his clothing. You can say it was the fear that spread like a disease during the war that made him this way… but I think he was this way all along which made him perfect war material…" Arthur broke off. He sounded tired now and the sun was hotter than any May he remembered.

"So did you come back here… together?"

"Yes we came here again… many years later on my 20th birthday, just Uncle Piero and me… he didn't have any children… Simon was five years younger than me and still at school in England. He took me round the shop on via di Fazzoletti… he explained a few things… I met a young Liza… and then we came up to Villa Angelo on his motorbike… and we just sat."

"You just sat? Did you sit where we are now?"

"Very nearly, the gardens were wilder then and there was no furniture. There were a few broken statues and the interior was a mess with damp and decay. It was abandoned during the war and overgrown with ivy and grasses. I'd not seen Uncle Piero through the war years, when I did, he'd lost weight and was a little yellow in the face and the colour in his eyes… I remember they had been an unusual blue… that had gone." Arthur paused, he played with a sandwich and then put it down again. "When we came back here I saw a little of the blue return to his eyes… it was as if he took some of the blue goodness from the sky. I could not face asking him about the war… everything I tell you now has been collected from others… other sources. We just sat together on this hillside of Fiesole and admired the view of a distant, seemingly unscarred Florence. It felt like the war had never come… that up here reality had been… well, I truly believe *it is*... suspended and only dreams and good things take place." Arthur paused again, perhaps he was being too poetical, maybe his romantic thoughts were racing ahead of him. He declined the sandwich Nina offered. "And you know," said Arthur matter-of-factly, "he didn't fight during the war because of poor eyesight. Although my mother always said he *was* fighting just not in a physical way."

"Sorry..." Arthur shook his head, "I just haven't said much, or any of this for... erm... a while. There seems a habit in our family of discovering the stories or the fates of those closest to you through other people... funny world eh? Sometimes I'm glad I know what I know and other times I feel so, ignorant."

"Is he still...?"

"He died in 1966... he was only 56. God! That's a year older than me," Arthur shook his head again, trying to throw off the years stuck to him. Being with Nina and telling an old tale played with his head; a clash of young and old at the same time.

"I'm sorry..."

"Well, that's how it is," said Arthur resolutely, shrugging his shoulders. "Uncle Piero was tired of life and smoked too many of these ugly things." Arthur tapped his pocket, put a half packet of cigarettes on the table and began to transfer the contents to his silver cigarette case. Nina recognised Arthur's actions as those of one who wanted to buy time to collect his thoughts.

She was thinking of Uncle Piero, he was very clear in her mind. "What a story he left behind... what frightening times to have lived through. It would have been impossible for him not to look back at the years of terror and fear of discovery… but being here with you must've been perfect medicine… coming here… a place you enjoyed together and… and at least the *Villa* wasn't damaged. Perhaps he could just allow himself some time to shut his eyes and remember life before the war…"

"Perhaps so… I'm afraid we can only imagine."

"Then I suggest… since all we can do *is* imagine, then we might as well," said Nina kindly and firmly, in a confident tone reserved only for a good friend and their closeness. If *she* had secured his openness then *he* must expect a clear and plain response.

"We might as well what?" Arthur seemed dozy.

"Imagine," said Nina. It was obvious what she was implying, wasn't it?

She was forthright, he thought, but he liked it; it suited her and maybe it was good for him to hear such a reaction but it wasn't just a reaction it was a new look at an old memory. She had been interested in him and listened and asked questions; she was inquisitive, she was unusual. At this moment, Nina could see the beneficial mix of her sensibilities and astuteness and Arthur's vulnerability and tenderness. It seemed to balance out their ages, Arthur reduced his years and Nina increased her years and thus their personalities allowed them to come together on equal terms, where age was not alike. She decided to not think about the age difference ever again and scrubbed it from her mind.

They sat in a silent reverie; a stillness echoed about the garden, too dry for birds and the bees had turned idle, even the leaves of the lemon bush began to wilt under the sun. The phantom waiter swiftly cleared the table and within minutes returned with two glasses of chianti.

"Chianti," whispered the waiter, which might have been the call of a bird if it hadn't been too hot for them. There was a little chattering from one of the tall side doors leading into the Villa like finely tuned sound effects for a radio drama.

A smartly dressed gentleman with a waistcoat stood within the loggia. He had a large nose and a bald patch and he looked across at Arthur, then patted a handkerchief neatly arranged in his top pocket. Arthur raised his scarlet-red wine and whispered to Nina, "Angelo the third… unmistakable." Nina glanced discreetly in the direction of Arthur's stare, but Angelo was gone, an Italian spirit vanishing behind the walls of the Villa.

After a sleepy hour under the parasol, drifting in and out of an afternoon's lazy spell, the long rays of the sun finally began to draw back their strength, bequeathing their power and energy to warm those below. Nina sat up with a start, convinced that this was the moment to tell *her* story. She had to show Arthur her handkerchief from the waving man and relate the unusual circumstances leading up to her ownership of this special piece of painted silk. She had not told anyone, she had sat with that wonderful and unaccountable feeling of strangeness and delight, and now she realised that on meeting Arthur those previous ill-defined emotions had been surpassed. With him she felt safe, and real and alive. Nina had brought the handkerchief to Florence and it was now sitting beside her in the little cloth bag she cherished, folded inside an envelope from the hotel

"Arthur," said Nina at first softly and then a little louder, "Arthur… Arthur… *look*…"

He awoke, gently rubbed his eyes, reached for his glasses and then froze.

"It's mine," said Nina. 'Um… it was a sort of gift.'

"*Yours?*" said Arthur astonished. He could not hide his incredulity which made him seem a little rude, but bewilderment can twist the tone of voice. He handled it very carefully and studied the design, the edges and the stitching. He ran his fingers over the painted roses, as Nina had done, and felt the texture of the silk between his fingers, then he passed it back to Nina with the warmest look in his eye. She felt relieved only because she had been tense, nervous even. Why, when a thousand thoughts must have flooded his head and crowded it all at once, did he remain silent? Aunt Merry would have seen flashes of providence and saintly blessings; signs and symbols flying above him; attributes in the forging of destiny. Then, unexpectantly, a common pigeon, much out of place and breaking the serenity, landed on the lawn and pecked greedily at some grass-seed.

"Well... I've seen a lot of handkerchiefs in my day." Arthur was feeling the old side of older again. "A gift? Well, well... as my father used to say."

"I know... it's your business." Nina didn't mean to ignore the reference to his father, but right now he wasn't part of this picture.

"Yes, it's just that this one was... well it belongs to my brother."

"Your brother?" said Nina, confused. Suddenly she felt upstaged. Arthur had told the incredible story of his Uncle Piero; was he to dominate her story as well? It was not his to own.

Arthur seemed mystified, "I haven't seen it for years... it was one I designed... faults sometimes appear in the stitching or the hand-painting isn't sale-worthy." Arthur bent to stand up and slid across to sit next to Nina, she'd been sitting on the two-seater white sofa. She felt a warmth spring from his body however she sensed a sudden strangeness, delivered by a startling set of fates.

He continued, "I liked this one... haven't seen it for years," he said again with a cough. Nina touched

Arthur's hand. She knew he wanted to know how she had come about owning it, and so naturally she followed through and told her story.

Villa Angelo seemed the very best place for stories, the telling and the making of them.

Part VIII

End of day

Arthur promised to call for Nina 'tomorrow.' He needed to return to the workshop and studio; discuss a series of new design ideas and, as he had told Nina before dropping her at the entrance to Antica Colonne, 'consider increasing our handkerchief selection.' He also said he needed 'to make a phone call too,' asking to keep her handkerchief, 'until next time.' He'd helped her off the bike and seen her into the hotel and suddenly he wanted to kiss her, not just a goodbye kiss but a kiss of tenderness and feeling. He realised he'd walked himself into the wrong place for such an intimate moment. The Villa would have been much more romantic but that was already an hour back in the past. Arthur wished he could have shown more feeling. He felt stuck and left awkwardly, annoyed with himself for being so absorbed by what had previously passed between them, instead of being more concerned with the present.

After what seemed such a momentous day for them both, Nina couldn't help but feel abandoned. There was no doubt Arthur's mind was distracted. He had just shared with Nina a family story long kept hidden. He'd been mildly surprised at his own openness. Then, out-of-the-blue she had revealed a handkerchief and suddenly several worlds were running at once. Any style of separation between the two of them would have felt like an anti-climax, it was too difficult to put an easy conclusion on the day. So, rather lethargically, with her own thoughts jumping over one another, Nina ascended the staircase. She noted her grumpiness, hiding it under the umbrella of 'tiredness.'

When Nina unlocked the door to the suite, a church bell sang six pretty peals, echoing down the Arno on the back of a swallow's wing. She sensed the window was slightly ajar allowing a light breeze to stir the tea-table and then heard some huffing and fumbling coming from Aunt Merry's room.

"Hello?" said Nina loudly.

"Oh... hello... it's me, I'm back..." came the fidgety cry of Aunt Merry. After an imaginative day Nina was relieved it was as simple as her aunt's early return.

"Are you all right? I thought you were going for a couple of nights?" Nina felt recharged at the sight of Aunt Merry. She was unpacking a small valise of light clothes, make-up and face-creams, eager to place them back on the shelves or in the comfort of the cupboards in which she felt they belonged. Aunt Merry detested empty spaces where items had previously sat, which is why when she came to the end of a face-oil or eye-cream there would always been another to re-fill its spot. She continued to rearrange her accoutrements while Nina flopped into a large lavishly upholstered armchair. It was a deeply comfortable piece of furniture and a long, long way from that white sofa at Villa Angelo. She moulded casually into its luxury.

"Wasn't quite what I was expecting. Not the places… just the company. I'm glad we left so early… some beautiful Tuscan country, yes… a few twisted roads, which I dealt with." Aunt Merry patted her head. "We went to Barga, Lucca and San Gimignano… all in a day. Oh! the olive groves… vineyards… ancient farmhouses… dusky mountains and monasteries… managed to pop my head round a few open doors. It really was splendid." There was a slight edge to her conversation, as if she might have found fault with something agreeable. Nina sensed the journey had, perhaps, uncovered something her aunt had not foreseen, and she did like to think she was prepared for most things.

"So what's the matter then?"

"Matter? Nothing." Aunt Merry said coolly.

"So why are you back early?" Nina persisted, "you had a room booked somewhere, didn't you?"

"Well it turns out there was a small room booked for Thaddeus and his friend in Barga and an even smaller room for myself and then I thought about this place." Aunt Merry sighed, looking around at her grand room with everything neatly arranged. She had even re-organised the items the chambermaid had dusted around. "And I thought about you… so I popped on the train and came back… just got in… well, ten minutes before you did. Anyway…" she wanted to change the subject, "where have you been today?"

Nina didn't want to change the subject. "Aunt Merry are you all right?"

"Yes, yes, much better now… the drive actually did me some good and the little towns were a joy. I now have a much clearer view of Tuscany… just what I wanted really. Are you hungry? I'm famished… these slippery, dusty old towns and their convoluted streets… I've not eaten… come on, let's go out!"

Nina, once again, admired her aunt's spirit. Aunt Merry had found Thaddeus a charming, genteel and interesting gentleman, qualities she had regularly recognised within the clergy. Only today she'd obviously discovered that Thaddeus' fellow touring companion was more than a friend. Sadly, she seemed both a little aggrieved and aggravated for not working it out, so she came back to Antica Colonne's offering of a large cosy bed and a good, filling Italian meal with Nina, who might lighten her evening with an interesting résumé of her own eventful hours.

"Let's go across the road to Osteria Mediterraneo… I could do with one of those ribollita soups," suggested Aunt Merry licking her lips in good humour, making Nina smile, allowing the atmosphere to relax once again.

They knew the restaurant and its menu well, and this alone reassured the two women, whose very different yet exhausting days needed the pacifying effect of comfortable food and a familiar and unchallenging evening.

They stood for 15 minutes for a specific corner table Aunt Merry had her eye on. It was near the back of the Osteria, tucked away in the quietest position. They were seated and presented with menus which Aunt Merry handed back to the waiter instantaneously. She ordered with confident vigour; firstly, two large glasses of house red, followed by two bowls of 'la zuppa ribollita.' A basket of thickly-sliced bread sprinkled in dry oregano, drizzled in a little olive oil arrived at the table. As soon as the wine came, Aunt Merry's spark was revived and she began to recall an amusing tale of her own. Something that had come to her, perhaps for no reason other than she was out in Florence with a long day behind her and with company she wanted to encourage.

"The first boyfriend I ever had took me to a small, French restaurant in London called, 'The Bon Gout.' He called it, The Bon Goat." Aunt Merry chuckled. "It was really a fancy fish and chip shop, there was nothing French about it at all… a few drippy candles in old wine bottles and checked tablecloths. He, Jimmy was his name, said the tablecloths and the napkins made it expensive. It was quite expensive, in those days going out was a real treat. Well, the tablecloths were plastic, sticky and smelt of vinegar. My mother, your grandmother, she was always so suspicious of things. She was suspicious of The Bon Gout, which made me feel slightly mischievous and wicked, but in a healthy rebellious sort of way... I see it now. I was only seventeen for goodness sake! It felt like the height of sophistication. Anyway, she said... your grandmother... she was suspicious of the restaurant title." Aunt Merry mimicked the high tones of her squeaky-clean mother, "the use and positioning of an English definite article with a foreign word is incorrect grammar... therefore if they cannot write properly, they cannot cook properly... it really is a waste of money. It suggests an amateur approach to cuisine... that the place can only have half an idea of what it's doing... either cooking or who it wants to attract..."

Aunt Merry returned to her tone, seeing a bit of sense in the reasoning but also remembering that the process of going out, of being out with a young man was no waste of time at all; it was life and freedom. "You know I think I enjoyed it more just because she thought this... 'The Bon Gout' I've never forgotten it! Anyway, Jimmy, 'the boyfriend!'" She chuckled again. "He spilt the vinegar bottle, he couldn't help it... it was leaky and you couldn't tell and we spent most of the funny meal dabbing the table with napkins and tissues... he was about to use his pocket handkerchief... he did look smart, he must have really been trying to impress... which was another of mother's suspicions... but I wouldn't let him."

Aunt Merry looked reflective and calm, poised with

her red wine and a serene smile. "I always liked genuine charm in a man and never liked vinegar, haven't touched it since... sometimes I think I can still smell it on my hands!" She laughed, and drained her glass just as the soups arrived; she ordered another glass of red. Nina indicated no-more for her. They ripped and dipped the bread into the soup in the style of pleased and thankful Italians. Nina felt the heat from the soup and the rosiness of the wine finally reach her toes. She too felt spurred on by food and by the odd little tale Aunt Merry had shared, there could be no better time to trust her senses and confide in her aunt. At some point, there often comes a point, when even hesitant and sensitive people find a happiness they long to safely reveal. She'd have to find the right words, Arthur deserved the best choice of words and perhaps talking about him would do some good.

Before coming to Florence, she had been directionless and lost; a change had been due her, although from where it might come and what it might be was always the uncertainty. Nina's head felt jumbled and she struggled internally with how to present her story. So, in true family tradition, she decided simply to throw herself in at the deep end of her thoughts and somehow work it all out from there.

"Aunt Merry, I've...I've... met someone... right here... and I think, well I'm in love... there I've said it!" She blushed with embarrassment, wondering how many surprises her aunt could take in a day, but this was her, Nina, her own niece, someone she had wanted to help; discoveries could come in all guises.

"Oh… I never loved Jimmy," said Aunt Merry, shaking her head and entirely missing the point. Then her eyes widened, she looked at Nina, blinked some moisture and re-took the conversation.

"Really?" Aunt Merry heard her pitch and tuned herself to a sensible, intimate, whispery level. "When did this… I mean, where… an Italian… in love?" She was remarkably quick at sobering up, years of ecclesial experience had done her an excellent turn. For an older woman, drinking, she was able to hold herself well and act masterfully in control of whatever situation she faced.

"You know I'm sure of it because I've never felt like this before… not once, not ever, not with one of those silly, immature 'boys'… anyway, he's not a boy, he's a… proper gentleman." Nina continued, happily on a roll for the first time about a man who actually warranted the attention. "He's called Arthur, he's half English, half Italian and he's the most interesting man I've ever met and I'm sure he likes me too. He's quite a bit older than me, but I don't mind that." Nina waved off the last remark, she'd closed the book on the topic of age and the age-gap.

"Well of course he likes you!" Aunt Merry blurted out excitedly, "you're young and very pretty and you're intelligent. What man wouldn't love such… such admiration."

Nina wasn't sure she liked her aunt's last observation. She made a mental reminder that the next time she met Arthur she would be sure to tell him of herself and make certain if he was to fall in love with her and attach strong, firm feelings to her, it would be for herself alone and not because she'd been such an ardent listener to his remarkable anecdotes.

So, to Aunt Merry's open eyes and brimming face, Nina recounted the last few days with Arthur. They had met at the English Cemetery and visited his shop on Via di Fazzoletti. Naturally intrigued, Aunt Merry had heard of the street mentioned but not taken the opportunity to give time to the district; 'not yet anyway… there's still time to wander that way.' Nina briefly described Villa Angelo in Fiesole, but not the story of Uncle Piero and not her own handkerchief. She was not in the habit of divulging all the mini-stories within one growing tale. Some things she knew were his and hers to own and, maybe these were the things that coupled a companionship into a relationship. As Nina came to a tired close and mulled over the story herself, she realised she didn't even know his surname. It had not come up. Arthur who? She wondered, and hoped keenly her aunt would not ask. Thankfully she didn't. Forgoing a homemade pannacotta soaked in a little marsala, which not even her sweet tooth could stay awake for, Aunt Merry paid the bill. She left a large tip which emblazoned a broad, shiny white smile onto the waiter's flushed face. It had been a longer day than intended, both ladies seemed relieved and relaxed to head back to the hotel and part for rest and sleep. Nina's light was out before her aunt's. Whatever the hour before bed, her aunt liked to perform a facial ritual of cleansing oat-milk creams, vitamin water-sprays and soothing juniper oils. The atmosphere of the room took on a warm, soothing aroma.

Nina lay in bed; she tossed and turned, at last settling her head in the centre of the pillow, looking up at a white ceiling shrouded by the darkness of night.

What was Arthur's surname? She must find out, she should know. What might it be? No matter. I do love him, all the parts I know and all the parts I don't and all there is to come. How much can anyone really know of a whole person? He's lived fifty-five years already without the slightest knowledge of me. What went before is past, I can do nothing to alter it; what comes next is unknown but what I do know is I want to be part of it.

Her head full of whirling questions gradually became sweetened by the soporific scents of lilac and lavender and she fell asleep.

Part IX

Talking to Arthur

'Feidling... Arthur Feilding... F.E.I.L.D.I.N.G,' read Nina. By ten a.m. the next morning a small envelope had arrived. It had not been slipped under the door of their room, it was placed upstairs on their breakfast table, a small, round, marble table lightly dressed in starched white linen: sturdy, heavy and impossible to move, most of all it didn't wobble. It was located in the best spot, a far corner of a long, narrow inside restaurant. No tables were set up outside. Aunt Merry liked tables in corners. She could see every guest enter and leave and they could see her. She liked to see them glance at her, she would then give a subtle wave, a wink or a friendly nod.

The top floor interior, overlooking the large terrace, had full-height, glass windows. Essentially front seats to the most commanding view of Florence and her beauty. The table was laid for Aunt Merry and Nina each morning. Even during her bout of illness Aunt Merry had made herself sit there and contemplate the skyline and will the wonders of Florence to remedy her and give life its shine again. Nina was first to see the envelope, resting between a glass and a teacup, 'For Nina, from Arthur Feilding.' He did not know her surname either but the sensible hotel receptionist had made sure the letter fell into the correct recipient's hand. Nina took some tea and juice and some dry, cooled toast and jam. Aunt Merry was ready to begin the morning afresh with a new detailed discussion on the topic of Arthur. She was also ready to make a clean break from yesterday's awkward sojourn with Thaddeus and his friend. It had always been her principle to leave behind incidences or quarrels or misunderstandings; brush them away, clear the day of them. Unfortunately the tension and minor rift between her and her sister had not found a resolution; blood may be thicker than water, but blood was bloody stubborn too.

Nina could sense the subject of Arthur building between careful bites and sips. She simply had to make her excuses and leave in order to read the message from Arthur alone and in private. It was sealed with red wax. Already she excitedly loved the idea of revealing the contents of the letter. Aunt Merry was sorry to see Nina leave so speedily, she thought she'd eyed a letter on the table. Her disappointment would not last long for she had decided to quiz the hotel manager, he was currently out on the terrace inspecting the health of the flower pots. She wished to discuss the peculiar smell of complimentary toiletries offered by the hotel and insist on suggesting they provide something, 'more ambrosial.' How might she present her ideas on the matter? Perhaps by suggesting orange blossom or lemon oil, something akin to the scents of Europe. This would be a stretch of her Italian tongue. There was a mandarin spray she had picked up in a Seville market a couple of years ago. On returning home she'd used the little concoction on an aeroplane flight and caused a sensation with fellow travellers as they attempted to find the person peeling an orange. The perfume had wafted all the way down the aisle, even the Spanish pilot was curious, local citrus wasn't yet in season!

Nina carefully undid her envelope from Arthur. The envelope and the notepaper were a matching clotted-cream colour. The sleeve of the envelope was designed in an elaborate pattern of twisted foliage of blue, red, yellow and green finished in gold and golden swirls, possibly stylised acanthus leaves intertwined with the great Florentine lily. It was flamboyant and beautiful; the paper version of a handkerchief. The note itself held a single red Florentine lily in the bottom centre surrounded by further colourful scrolls, baroque spirals and curling volutes.

Written with a thick, black fountain-pen, Nina read cautiously:

'My sweet Nina, you have inspired me and given me a lot to think about. I've not felt like this in a long while.

I must be careful what I write, my mind seems to flow but my pen suggests I must hold back. I wish I could find better words but at present they fail me. I am not as well versed as my ancestors. I see I have been very selfish and talked solely of myself knowing little of you. I know only the effect you have on me.

I will pass by tomorrow at 11. A day later than I thought. I hope you don't mind if I intrude on your holiday. There is something quite special between us I believe. I hope you feel the same. I have my doubts, for obvious reasons. Now you see, my pen has been let loose! With fondness, Arthur'

A tingling sensation ran down Nina's spine. She was so conscious of the reaction of her body to his words. How beautifully he had written, his lines, a form of poetry. They were words directed to her. She had had an influence over this man, just by being herself. She felt dizzy with both wonder and fear, then sensed these two feelings hit one another and cancel out the effect and meaning of each; she resolved to become her normal self again. She realised from her own life experiences, it was not an easy thing trying to be your natural self in the world. There was envy, jealousy and competition. There were lies, made and spread, and superficiality. She had to stop thinking negatively; it was a ridiculous way to think when everything seemed to be in her favour. She had been looking for change and love had come along; love can change people.

The following day came and Nina met Arthur in the hotel hallway at 11am, as he had suggested. He was sitting on an ornately upholstered chaise-longue; one, female Carrara marble nude in Venus pudica stance stood to his left. Arthur looked relaxed. Nina took a minute from the staircase to admire him. Any other man she'd known might have been embarrassed, out of place and bemused. Arthur looked comfortable, unphased. He sat amongst art as an artist does, understanding its beauty and giving appreciation. It was part of his life and upbringing. He was accustomed to it. He was clear and bright. Other men she'd known seemed juvenile, smug, arrogant in their ignorance. Whether people knew Arthur or not, his presence heralded recognition. From her secluded position she thought on the letter he had written; it had made her feel special. She loved how she benefitted from his esteem, if he was so well-regarded then she could reflect a little in his glory.

Nina wandered over and greeted him with a kiss. She was so glad to see him.

"Thank you for your note... it was lovely," Nina said. Arthur bowed lightly in response.

"Let's go up to the terrace... come see the view... we won't be disturbed up there, most of the guests have gone out."

"Whatever you like," said Arthur, following. His voice was croaky. Had he not slept? Had he regretted writing so hastily? So much was playing on his mind. Nina's imagination was kept busy skipping from one idea to the next, just because he'd uttered those words.

She called the lift. Nina was more nervous today, more so than any of the other times with Arthur. Why was that? Was it because he'd expressed something intimate; because he'd revealed his feelings toward her? Was she expected to do the same?

"Where is your aunt today?" asked Arthur, it was a simple question and eased Nina fluidly into conversation.

"She's gone to San Marco, to the museum, Fra Angelico's work... there's a very beautiful Annunciation... she likes to wander along the corridor, peering into the cells and contemplating the frescoes and the little wooden windows with the light pouring in... She finds it enormously peaceful. Last time we went... the noise from the streets set our ears ringing. Once we were inside, we adjusted to the silence. She said that in the deep vacancy all she could hear was choral music. You know," said Nina reflectively, "it did seem so."

"She sounds like a very spiritual lady."

"Oh she is! She was a vicar's wife, twice over. Now she helps out in church, occasionally, particularly in therapy. She has many insightful skills."

"Like you... you're very perceptive... intuitive... all these." Arthur added swiftly, "I mean it as a good thing."

"With the right people I am," said Nina and she smiled.

"Liza told me she thought you were and I agreed."

Their conversation was that of an overture preparing them for a more settled location.

With Arthur's years and knowledge, he wasn't going to frighten her. The approach with Nina would have to be right. Writing was a form she would like. Anyone searching out a poet on the outskirts of Florence was someone seeking another soul: a lover of words, of language, of spontaneity, maybe even passion and rebellion.

They sat on a large, low, informal sofa and gazed at Brunelleschi's Duomo. What an architectural marvel. The citizens of Florence would have gazed in awe at this feat of engineering. Looming and towering above them soared God's work and below scurried his congregation going about their daily business with faith and belief until He saw fit to steal them away to his Kingdom where they too would be raised high into the sky.

Arthur and Nina stared through the freshly wiped glass windows without a word for many minutes. There was the clink of glasses being placed on a high shelf and the sound of a bar being re-stocked but there was no human chatter or murmur, just the closeness of efficiency. The urgent city sounds were far away, their echo subdued by layers of interior kindness. Nina knew so well every angle of Il Duomo, she could see it in her inner eye; when asleep, when walking, it was a pink silhouette. It was a sight she was sharing with Arthur and she saw it as a heart, a symbol of their meeting. Nina stood up and filled two glasses with plain water, at least the table was being put to function and the scene between them would look convivial. She was not the kind of person for whom opening up and talking about herself was straightforward. In this case it was not the company, Arthur would be easy to talk to, it was how to go about it.

Her predisposed theory of being a guarded person was mostly based on the reasoning that if you did speak plainly about matters close to you, then someone may later use this to hurt you, as she had found amongst school-friends and later work-colleagues. It was complicated to explain but these sensitivities did stem from experience. However, Nina knew she was the only one holding herself back. Comfortable and calm with Arthur beside her and with a mild apprehension, she began. She knew, as most people do, one is inextricably linked to the dramas of one's life so far and although the past cannot determine the future there is no doubt it can form a pattern.

Nina's father had left the family; her younger sister and mother, Mrs Hurst, when she was seven years old. She pointed out almost light-heartedly her surname was Hurst. He had given no warning, and there was no further contact.

There were only two significant memories Nina could recall of her father. One was a fancy-dress birthday party when he'd come disguised as a large, white rabbit which instead of delighting the children had thrown them into fits of screams and terror. It had been an ambitious idea which had definitely fallen short of the right effect. The other was when his giant furniture lorry, the length of three buses, got stuck in a snow-drift outside their detached suburban house. The driver had misjudged the fore-warned weather conditions and the consequences of a narrow, kerbed road with bushes. The neighbours turned a blind eye, little could be done and seeing it was close to Christmas, people forgave most things especially when bottles of mulled wine were offered in apology. The lorry was expecting to make a country-wide delivery of three-piece suites and armchairs but the orders would not reach their owners this side of the new year. Nina's father opened up the back of the lorry. The furniture was covered in slippery hard plastic. Nina and her sister crept into the container load and spent happy hours climbing from one set of sofas to other, jumping them like horses in a race and playing hide and seek in the weak light. When their father came back, he found two little girls had removed the nasty plastic covering and had snuggled themselves down into the gap between the sofa seats. He was not cross, he was never cross, but he was always distant, always looking beyond their faces as if he saw another life waiting for him. And then one day it was strong enough to pull him away; he took it and was gone.

At her very conventional school, she had very conventional friends and thus found herself to be one of a kind, having just a mother and no father.

Immediately she did not fit into a mould. This made her susceptible to attack from school-girls who lived ordinary lives with their ordinary parents in pleasantly-lit streets with rose-beds encircled with lavender bushes in a perfect middle England setting. As soon as the time came, Nina's secondary education and mother's family roots took the girls to London. Here a new set of issues would line her path and she learnt how much she liked one to one interaction and really disliked large groups or cliquey girl clans.

When she moved to working in the city's museums, all her associates were foreign. When new recruits came to her department, she found herself introducing a German to a Swiss, a Swiss to a French etcetera and subsequently as the weeks rolled by, she found she was being left out of the European equation in her birth country. In a city as exciting and important as London she felt remarkably lonely amongst her peers.

Poetry, reading and writing, became a solitary pastime, not in any way a serious profession. Nina had considered and then reconsidered the idea of turning her pleasure into a job. Inevitably it would make it a chore, the mystery would be spoiled. She didn't want her hobby of poetical writings to be spurned, criticised or critiqued. In a chance meeting she had fallen upon a fledgling publisher and paid a sum towards the printing of a small book of her best collection. In poetry she could touch on any theme or any manner of characters. Expressing an element of her vulnerability mixed with a deep imagination, inspiration came from time spent alone or wandering and travelling. Stopping to observe the world around her, she found emotions were broad and wide.

Nina knew she had never been in love. There had been the idea of love and infatuation, which was as dangerous as a drug for it was false love, never true love. Nina could not bring herself to speak too openly to Arthur on love. She knew without a doubt she'd found love with him. It was difficult to describe, she understood why poetry was such a good medium. True, reciprocated love made you shine and glow; she felt like a better version of herself, stronger and wise.

Nina's father rarely entered her head to trouble her. She was happy to leave him in the past, if he'd chosen not to return then why should she return constantly to him? In poetry she could present problems, solve them or not, but at least set them on the page, to read or discard.

Leaving London once again, older and more resilient, Nina turned to journalism. This writing style was more fluid and factual and had offered a multitude of issues. She'd worked with easy-going and less challenging or aggressive people. Lately she'd found her intuition had attracted the oddest scenarios and a strangeness that had made her feel she was living in another layer of life. Aunt Merry might have been the best person to confide in, having what she herself called 'a spiritual discernment,' but Nina had recently kept her tendencies tight to herself. She thought how peculiar all this might sound to Arthur. She did feel very free in his company despite her usual cautious self and suddenly that directionless and disillusioned girl was being discovered.

During Nina's monologue Arthur had listened with great interest and urgency. Yes, urgency was right. He had believed her to have held something unique; he'd trusted her with stories dear to him, the fabric of his life. When she had presented him with a handkerchief he had once kept close to his heart, it confirmed there was nothing ordinary about their coming together.

Of late Arthur had felt listless and tired; his routine, though interesting to others, was proving monotonous. In Nina there was a freshness, a vitality and a spirit.

To travel to Florence had been an excellent idea. Nina did not expect it to be as idyllic as poetry devises or as music composes, or even as tremendously savage as a playwright may choose but oh just to feel something of the romantic joy she had so often penned.

Arthur had heard and absorbed Nina's words. It was clear she loved his presence but was still slightly wary in her way. She had looked between him and Il Duomo, attentive lest any disturbance should come.

"Would you like some more water?" Arthur was unsure how to help her end comfortably. She looked drained and a bit tearful, as if she was intending to keep sunk some bothering emotion.

Without realising it she had drained her water glass.

"Um… no I'm fine," was her dull response.

"Fine is not good, I'll get you some." Arthur got up slowly. It was odd. They both suddenly felt bereft not sitting side by side after the intimacy of the past and of the constant present. It was those small stabs of feeling that were the workings of love. Nina had existed so long without certain sensations, to feel them now was another strangeness.

Nina was sharply brought back to the moment with the unexpected and rather embarrassing arrival of Thaddeus and his companion. She raised a perfunctory hand, it was rather automated, like a reflex, but a polite thing to do. Her Aunt Merry had been at a loss for words in her understanding of Thaddeus and his friend. She'd claimed, in fact, to be a modern woman and really was, yet was still affected by what she called 'the unfathomable.'

Arthur placed the glass of water down and touched Nina's shoulder. She wanted him to kiss her. When the room quietened down once more, a distinctively musical Florentine chime hung in the air. This time Nina failed to count the bells, Arthur leaned in to kiss her, his hand on her chin.

Part X

Simon's story

It was walkable, the distance from the large auction house of Duke Street St James, to a notable, public place of sanctuary. Simon had pin-pointed one great space of refuge and would make his way there, eventually. In the meantime, a little song and dance would do the trick and he'd lose his followers easily. He knew London well: the side-streets, the back roads, the old theatre alleyways. The persistent rain would make his stride across town an added hindrance. He would have to dodge the urban hazards, use the architecture and the city people all to his advantage, for the situation he now found himself in was precarious, even dangerous.

All the great auctions of 20th century London had taken place under the roof of the Duke's vast building, earning a sizeable fortune from a succession of popular annual sales. Currently, on a public scale, there was the competitive desire to display the rarest and finest works of art, spawned by the appetite of nationwide museums and galleries. In private, the rise of Art as a fashion accessory and a safe investment for funds was undisputed.

Today, a wet, grey, February day, a small auction of personal treasures had taken place in one of the more modest rooms of Ducks, as it was affectionately known. The story of how it became Ducks depended on the teller. The more pragmatic would say it was a corruption of the word Duke, taking the following 's' from Street to pluralise it. The more rakish stories came from the 1800s; one favourite was when a wealthy baronet bought himself a duck-house from one of the more curious auction-sales. He was supposed to have asked, in the smoothest of voices, if they could provide him with the ducks to complete the purchase. Rumour had it two ducks were 'procured' and the same lineage of duck has continued to bless the stately home's duckpond ever since, although no one person at Ducks could tell you *which* stately home.

Another such tale existed when the building closed suddenly due to swans from the nearby Royal park settling their seven cygnets comfortably under the House's awnings. Flash flooding and loss of land had forced them to find shelter and it took two weeks, with a copious amount of free summer publicity, before they moved back to their roots. Although, some argued, they were not ducks, they had used the safety of the house to 'duck out' of inclement weather. The papers had a field day of 'ducking-swan jokes.'

Nonetheless. As far back as the oldest surviving employee, everyone knew the Auction house as Ducks, the name had stuck.

Let's return to a windowless, internal room, the walls covered in finely coordinated fabrics, presenting to the buyer just the right combination of comfort and unquestionable good taste. Hundreds of carefully positioned lights were in place to perfectly illuminate each piece of art. The sale, entitled 'Mid-20th century decorative curiosities,' was a combined selection of artefacts accumulated by three wealthy and eccentric, matriarchal, dynastic families. After the clearing of debts and taxes and family confrontations and appeasements, it had taken over four years to gather and catalogue the sale contents and to subsequently and exclusively publicise the event.

Simon, as foretold, had his eye on Lot 32, a handkerchief of the Italian style circa early 1940s. How, his brother Arthur, had come to trace its whereabouts after 48 years, remained a mystery. Simon, a man of few questions and few answers respectfully, did not pry. He knew the art-world was like the ocean – one day it would churn up a treasure, you just had to know *what* it was you wanted and to keep looking in all the right places.

It was Arthur who'd suffered the greatest trauma when the Heinegette family were captured.

The handkerchief was described briefly on page 77 of the glossy catalogue as a green silk, hand-painted handkerchief, hand-stitched edging, faded colouring and lettering, several indistinguishable marks or stains. The description was short and basic; such items were not regularly sold. Ducks was clearly reliant on the families alone for a good sell, for provenance 'mysterious past' would be sufficient to fetch a healthy sum. He had spent half an hour that morning examining the specimen, trying to quash his excitement, knowing what he knew this handkerchief to be. He would have to wait patiently, relax his muscles and most of all, use British sophistication and charm to bluff his way through the elaborate and formal sale proceedings. He was so pleased Arthur had set him such a mission this year. At first he thought Arthur better for the task, but in retrospect Arthur was too romantic, too attached, too generous, too readable. Simon was capable of disappearing if needs be, and resurfacing without really being missed. He was a man people always believed they'd met before, which made him both distinguishable and yet also allowed him to hold a secretive individuality.

Simon had expected some trouble at the beginning of the auction when two burly men, uncomfortable in their ill fitting suits, had entered the sale room just as the first lot was called. One held the thin catalogue of sale and the other a paddle. They took the right attributes yet Simon had his suspicions and he was particularly jumpy himself. He had awoken with a headache, his facial pressure-points seemed stressed. He was feeling wary, or rather he felt made to feel wary by some looming presence of intimidation.

Now, yards from his seat, stood made-to-order men, paid recruits, brawny mercenaries. Counterbalancing their physical weight, Simon reassured himself they may not be swift or smart and that he was resolute and impassioned. They had a look of dark, steely determination; their eyes reflected the hard light, giving them a menacing turn. These men were a warning to Simon. Instinctively he knew they were after the same simple object as he, which means someone else knew of its importance.

The auction was nearing its end; the sale of the handkerchief was brief. He out bid one meagre woman and one phone bid. The men made no offers. Their employer was not keen to purchase the handkerchief, they were clearly there to steal it from whomever the purchaser might be: that person, as the gavel sounded its solid stamp of approval, was Simon.

A long, final twenty minutes of heated deliberations, and frenzied back and forth bids in the small enclosure stifled the room and allowed the men to focus on their target. Simon slipped out of the room via the door closest to him. He took the staircase, three flights down to the basement to avoid queues, interaction, and to pay the final sum and collect his item, hurrying the chatty girl with a practised politeness. It was already neatly wrapped and packaged in a box emblazoned with Ducks' logo: a feather. He checked the parcel, placed it carefully and discreetly in his inner pocket and left the box and ribbons much to the disappointment of the girl. He went to the cloakroom, collected his coat and hat and headed for the main exit. By now the central lobby was full of people, all shapes and sizes, their discourse filled the upper air as much as their bodies clung to the carpets. The space was swallowed up. Simon carefully negotiated his way through a maze of garments, handbags and loose limbs.

Despite the crowding, Simon caught sight of the two men preparing to pursue him. In an instant they had locked eyes. One look invoked fear. Whoever *he* was, the handkerchief would be in *their* hands by the end of the hour.

Simon's composure was tested.

So now we follow Simon and the London he walked into that late morning. He was smart and level-headed, he had to be. Thinking on the go, inventing the next step, planning a route and then changing it, it was crucial to act for the sake of his precious possession and its secure delivery. He would not allow them to interfere, or worse still, consider killing the carrier. The more open and alive his environment, the safer and stronger he felt.

The gutters quickly became channels of water. The drains became blocked with twigs and old foliage, the pools expanded, as wide as ponds and a foot deep making them impassable even with a leap. He switched direction. The edges of his coat soaked up the water, a dark brown fringe weighed his pace. He continued until The Haymarket, turning his head just once. He glimpsed the smudged outline of two men. They were more active than he thought and realised he had convinced himself of their ineffectualness too easily. He safely boarded a route-master bus bound for The Aldwych. Where might he escape to next?

Congestion and pedestrians forced the bus to pull slowly around Trafalgar Square. Simon tested his inner pocket for the parcel; he checked his outer red handkerchief and attempted to shake off some of the rain from his hat. An older, well-dressed lady, immaculate and as dry as a bone sat beside him with armfuls of shopping. She handed him a pouch of tissues which he courteously accepted with a silent nod. She was immune to the weatherly pitfalls facing the city outside. She watched him pat down his clothing as if he had brought about the rain and its mess himself. The bus call-bell sounded sharply and Simon disembarked at Charing Cross. Leaving the liquified and polluted air of the main station entrance he kept his eyes low and headed for the steps to the underground. He was aware he was being followed by the burly men and by other commuters, which was a chase of another sort. As Simon picked up his pace along the dirty station tunnel so did those other commuters, as if he knew something they didn't, as if the faster he walked the quicker a train would come, but he wouldn't take a train. He'd fool them all and turn off at an alternative exit, a set of steps that led back up into Trafalgar Square. He wanted to be in a mixture of people, somewhere frantic and frenetic. Simon's hot nerves began to calm a little as he reached the top curving step. Here he entered a throng of scattering, umbrella-wielding city escapees, with a wild sense of direction. Very suddenly and dramatically, and gulping at the realisation he seemed to stand-out all too easily. He was all too recognisable. He couldn't blend into the murky background as he had anticipated and just as this very fear caught his brain, he realised the two men were close by. He could feel their eyes burn into the back of his neck. So instead, he played an opposite game. Having placed himself amongst people in order to hide, he now decided, since it was possible, to set himself apart and draw attention to himself by waving to someone, anyone far enough away, looking directly south towards his position. If he could cause a momentary distraction, force his presence into the grimy limelight, it might appear to his followers he was not alone, that he had a friend, a companion, a second accomplice and he was giving them a signal. The hired men would have to back down, abandoning their hope for a quiet brawl. They might have hoped for a quiet brawl in a wind-swept, deserted park. With Simon beckoning to some significant mark on the landscape the threatening men wouldn't come near him and risk being so visual. For whatever they planned to do with Simon, they had no idea what he had planned. He was clearly smarter and braver prey than they had reckoned.

Simon waved vigorously. The curled brim of his fedora hat nodded in support of his provocation. The next few moments depended on a make-believe thought, a bit of play-acting, just to buy him some time to make a speedy, wet rush across the square to his chosen safe-house, The National Gallery. In the warmth and protection of its wood-polished floor and comforting interior and its impressive collection, he would be able to catch his breath and gather his ideas. A sense of achievement and the fulfilment of a task could not be fully felt until the handkerchief was clean away, innocently in transit. He continued to wave until the damp seeped into his shoulders, long enough to make him feel uncomfortable and, most significantly, identified. Far off, someone *had* seen him and responded. As he persisted in waving at the gallery's portico entrance, he could feel the slow and reluctant departure of two sets of dense eyes and their weary bodies. They sank back into the underground, as if to sink back into the underworld, rats into the sewers. For now, one wave had saved him.

Simon, who seemed to gain energy while others faltered, then darted through the square to the gallery, free of the weight of pursuit. He knew he needed to work quickly and to free himself of this undertaking. He was glad he had been so pre-prepared and addressed a parcel to *'Firenze, Italia.'* Once in the dry he could scribble a note to his brother who should receive the item by April when he arrives to start up the business again. Two months or more between the Ducks' auction and sale to Simon and Arthur's discovery of the parcelled handkerchief was, he hoped, long enough to cut links with any dangerous interest.

The hired men had given their last chase. Tired from exertion, they were willing to take the tirade of abuse from a paying foreign boss, whose false monies and fraudulent accounts would not buy this favour. Their time in this job would end today. They were no fitter, nor wiser and ultimately, they would wonder why were they hunting this man in the first place. It was clear an emotional attachment always outweighed a monetary value. In an old pub after hours they'd think up an unconvincing yarn of bravura and bravery to present to their dark employer. Even he, however angry, would have to agree his hapless recruits could not outsmart or overpower the strong will of a masterful adversary. There were new tricks being played in the world of deception; movements were becoming more watched and traced, actions were recorded and analysed. There were eyes everywhere and although this work had always been unsafe and uneasy, the risks outweighed the rewards. Let it go, let it end today.

For the remainder of the afternoon Simon kept alert, with a stubborn tension in his shoulders that refused release. Wandering through the rooms of the gallery with an artificial attentiveness he found the warmth from the painted canvases and the embracing atmosphere gradually allowed the tightness in his features to ease.

He thought of the old handkerchief in his inner pocket and what a special prize it was. The soft silk seemed to settle thankfully beside his heart, beating out its' symbol of courage, faith and endurance; proud of its role as an object of talent, bravery and most of all freedom. What an extraordinary past it had had and now it would return home once more to the street where it was made, Via di Fazzoletti. Not to be sold and not to resurface again, not in Simon and Arthur's lifetimes. Their family would now silently and sacredly possess it. It would be buried by time. So these are the thoughts of the present, for those who pick up the future are the yet unknowns.

Well before five o'clock arrived, Simon had brushed up his appearance, rearranged his coat, hat and clothing and brightened up his signature red handkerchief. His unblemished bronze complexion had returned after a morning of shadowy white edginess. He was feeling bright, courteous and happy on a new, healthy dose of adrenaline: a job nearly done. He made his way to the large, main Post Office near St Martin-in-the-Fields and waited for the old-rural chimes of five. As he completed the final postal requirements his eye was caught by the entry of the young girl who, in his moment of need, had returned his energetic waving. This, he decided, was the closure of the circle. *Something* seemed to link the two of them. He didn't know why *she* of all people had returned his wave. Suddenly she sneezed and he knew to give her his red silk handkerchief, whispering, 'bless you' as he passed.

With the parcel deposited and ready for flight, and now with a renewed inner spirit of euphoria, who knows what he might do?

Part XI

Leaving Florence

Humming an operatic tune her ears had picked up from an open window in an inconspicuous alleyway days ago, Aunt Merry packed away her oil bottles and cream jars. She wrapped them tightly and snuggled them amongst her clothes bags and shoes and numerous souvenirs. Interspersed between improvised musical notes her mind was slowly making a proverbial change from scenes in Florence to situations in Winchelsea, her home.

"Seed planting," she exclaimed, "flowers for the display!"

If you'd been bothered to piece her cries into understandable sentences, which Nina was not, her aunt was lamenting (a dramatic habit she had picked up from the Tuscans) over her flower-pots and plants and promises for the church summer fete and the congregational flower arrangements. She had set the annual colour theme for the year: red, white and blue. One of the Toms from St Thomas' had offered to water and attend to her garden. It was kind and she had accepted with alacrity, but he would not dead-head the pansies or see-to the trailing petunias and each were susceptible to her slug and snail-ridden garden. She couldn't leave instructions; it would seem rude and presumptuous. Aunt Merry fiddled with her postcards, selecting two from The Uffizi, she scribbled a thank-you note to two Toms, she couldn't recall which one she'd asked. Life back in England felt three months old not three weeks. It would be one less job to do when home and despite feeling concerned for what she might discover when she returned, she was, in general, most generous in thought. Within days of being back, Florence would seem like a distant memory, the mental clouds folding over their holiday, much like the real ones shading the glory of the sun.

Leaning her head out of the hotel window, Nina was asking herself question after question, inventing probable answers; it was horrible. She was leaving today; she had said so to Arthur: *in the late afternoon.* Where was he, why didn't he remember? What about *her* red handkerchief? He had not returned it; he hadn't said anything. And there was something else, something he wasn't telling her, perhaps he was just confused, preoccupied. There are other things besides *you* in his life. She knew this, but their friendship had quickly become something newly felt and he'd encouraged it. All she could think about was Arthur, the possession she'd cherished before meeting him and how mysteriously it belonged to his brother; or so he said. How had this happened? Soon she would be gone. Where was he?

She hated how she felt. As those provoking questions mounted in Nina's head, she'd feel stabs to the heart and tears begin to well in her eyes, as every soft and sensitive part of her body became affected.

Nothing made sense anymore. Why wasn't she full of happiness? Her recent touch of joy, disappearing from her soul as rapidly as the suntan after a holiday. She felt sick. It would have been better if he'd never come along at all, for the injury she felt, right at that very moment, was insufferable.

Aunt Merry was aware Nina was upset; emotion and body-language are not easy to hide from a close companion. There was little she could do or say. By the afternoon they would both be gone from Florence and yet it would not be just the city Nina would be leaving behind. Love was such a delicate subject. She had buried her heart in his lap and was struggling to retrieve not just her sense but her whole self. If Nina wanted to talk to her aunt she would always listen, she had listened before. Aunt Merry called out to say she was taking the lift to the terrace for tea before returning to pack more of her items and trinkets. Nina had a hunch she was looking for new company, that she, Nina, had become dull and unresponsive. She'd tried to hide her upset with a few interjections of interest and placation; she was not one to ignore Aunt Merry. Nonetheless the triviality of her plants was nothing compared to an aching heart

England seemed like a country she did not know, whereas Florence seemed to hold so much.

Aunt Merry came out of the bathroom with a gift-wrapped soap and a floral room spray. Deciding to keep the perfumeries for herself, she lay them down on a nearby table and opened the suite door to leave.

"Nina dear, you can spend all day at that window… *try* to focus on something else… do try, my dear. Florence and the Arno won't be there tomorrow." The door hissed in agreement as it closed.

Her vision had been too narrow. So she blinked, refreshed her watery eyes and focused hard.

Down below on the other side of the River Arno was a typical Italian coffee and ice-cream café. It was close enough she could make out the comings and goings of people. She watched them, walking in, walking out, making decisions, passing by, little groups buzzing about the long windows, choosing and chattering. Italian businessmen would throw back a hot espresso in seconds; children came for lunch-time gelati, chirping and jumping about. It was called 'Spuntini.' The 'u' in the word was a crescent smile with a tongue, licking an ice-cream. Nina had seen it before, yet this time she wanted to observe it properly and thoroughly, to take her mind out of the silly state it was in. If she could think on one simple place, it would force her anxieties over Arthur to cool, then she would feel decidedly better. It was a sensible theory. *'Try* to focus on something else,' her aunt had said.

On returning home she'd be able to recall the image of 'Spuntini' beside the river, basking in a high sun on all corners, with a cooling blind and small round tables, with a 'specials' board; receiving customers with smiles, and they departing in sweetness. When her head was full of the next phase of life it would be a welcome tonic. Nina could feel the sting of her dry eyes, the pang of pain pass over and her strength and resolution slowly return. Although she was none the wiser or happier, some of the previous anger had subsided. And then quite suddenly and still entirely focused, she spotted Arthur. Tall and broad in his linen trousers and jacket, a customary handkerchief in his top pocket, he removed his brimmed hat and entered 'Spuntini.' About five seconds later two young women joined him. Their intimate gestures suggested they all knew one another well. The girls were English-pale, quite tall in long jeans and loose tops; similar in features, probably sisters, though not twins. What were they doing in Arthur's company? At first sight of him, Nina felt discomfited and a return of that burn in her heart she'd been trying to extinguish. Seeing him in character, seeing him stride confidently into the shade and pull round three chairs, she wanted to love and hate him at the same time. Who were these girls? He was so close and yet so far away. The same man yet *who* was this one? The questions started up again. This day was already too long, so she shut her eyes. She hoped by banishing her sight it might increase her hearing; the power of one sense over the other when one is lost. The reverberations came close; the swallows swift wind-on-the-wing sound, the pigeon coo, the hoot of cars and bicycle whistles, the ringing of bells. Then came the accents and harmony of language, mostly an animated vowel-absorbed Italian, some energetic Spanish, some dull, heavy

German, a little pedestrian English, which the ear picks at, automatically sensing the lyrics. She could not hear Arthur. She knew his deep voice but it did not reach her ears across the water. It could not get to her as he would not come for her. Why was he sitting opposite the Antica Colonne, *her* hotel, with *two girls?* Nina's stubborn mind persisted. He was a thoughtful man, wasn't he? It was thoughtless not to come to her and twice as tormenting to see him with these *two girls.*

Nina closed the window, and the curtain and forcibly shut out the light, with a second determined tug of the heavy drapes. She lay on her bed and wished for rain and grey, shadowing clouds and if possible, thunder and storms. She wanted people to feel the cold of disappointment; a gate that blocked happiness from streaming over your soul. She wanted a dramatic deluge to drive people indoors to end their outdoor pleasures, and for lightning to cackle in hysteria across the sky, mocking those who thought love was a never-ending wonder. She was sick of the sun and the heat and the endless, deep celestial blues on which lovers float their dreams.

The next thing Nina heard, loud and persistent, was the telephone in her aunt's room. She answered but too late to catch the caller. She washed her face and checked her watch, only a half hour had passed; in her confusion and anguish it had felt like three days. What did she feel now? She couldn't remember. As she descended the stairs to reception to inquire about the call, little visions of her emotions forty minutes earlier began to be re-played. By the time she'd reached the Lobby, there was Arthur. He sat on the chaise-longue looking so handsome and attractive, he had caught more of the delightful Florentine sunshine. Once again when their eyes met Nina felt a prick of love.

"Hello," she said, reserved but secretly so happy.

"Hello again," said Arthur cheerily.

"I'm leaving today," said Nina in her matter-of fact manner, sitting down beside him, watching his expression sadden.

"Yes, I'm sorry to hear that, I hadn't forgotten… and I'm sorry I'm late, I got caught up in some business."

"Oh, I suppose that happens all the time… I mean, I wondered if you'd come at… well I mean I just wondered," Nina said coolly, but very gladly.

"I most definitely *was* going to come," Arthur said honestly and defensibly, "without question… and not just because I'm returning the red handkerchief… but because I wanted to… er…" Arthur fumbled for a small, brown, padded envelope and handed it to Nina. She placed it next to her as if its return didn't really matter, what mattered was listening to him and sitting with him.

"I spoke to my brother…"

"Simon?" said Nina, she knew. She wanted to be involved and connected; to be a character entangled in a tale; to be part of one of Arthur's absorbing stories.

"Yes... we talked a bit yesterday evening... he said he'd felt a combination of relief and joy, his mission accomplished and this made him... well... generous, so he'd handed it to a girl, in the..."

"In the St Martin-in-the-Fields post office?" said Nina, and to herself, so Simon was the waving man; how peculiarly wonderful!

"Yes, just as you told me. He was posting a parcel to me that day... a very special handkerchief. When I came out in April, there it was safely waiting for me," Arthur swallowed, "I'd been delayed coming out... anyway what a..."

"What an extraordinary coincidence!" they chorused together and smiled.

"Well yes... but then again... it only makes me believe something more," Arthur said with conviction.

"What?" This time Nina held back, she wasn't going to put *her* words into *his* mouth, but surely, they felt the same.

"Well... that we were *always* meant to meet... and that we'll *always* know one another..." Arthur smiled again; Nina felt transfixed by her feeling of love. "My address is in the parcel... write to me first, if you feel happy to, and I will write to you and... soon I will come and see you in England... very soon. I want us to become... closer."

"I thought you had to stay *here* at the shop?"

"Yes, but I can get away!"

"And become close to me?" said Nina, checking him with his own words.

"Yes," said Arthur, "exactly, if you like. I have another motorbike in England, we can take some rides... there must be many beautiful lanes in Sussex and sunsets to see."

"I love the idea and... and even if we don't do it, the fact that you've suggested it means..."

"Oh, we *will* do it, no doubts," Arthur was certain, he looked directly into her eyes and held her small hands in his. They sat happily side by side. It would not be an easy affair. They would try and work it out, carefully; for something so beautiful deserved the best chance.

Why could they not part like this? Blissfully cheerful, blushing, kissing, besotted, all the buoyant and bright words, clustering together to describe their union. Why? There was a niggling sensation in Nina's ears. Who were the two girls she saw, cosy with Arthur? Who were those two girls, giggling and cuddling him? And then, with mind and mouth in sympathetic accord, Nina said quietly,

"Who are those two girls you were with today... at 'Spuntini'... across the river?"

Arthur found she'd dropped his hands; the sun in his heart suddenly obscured.

He had nothing to hide and yet by omission he had hidden a very significant detail about himself. It was not one he thought could possibly affect her and neither would he let it. He'd been so excited and overturned by the present that other subjects of his past hadn't been explained. Suddenly they'd come to the forefront and he needed to set the scene to rights.

"Ah," said Arthur, "those two girls are my daughters..."

"Your *daughters*?" said Nina, edging back from Arthur, seeing a new light fall on him; a new angle from her static pose. She looked a little hurt, and in her third breath, slightly relieved.

"Yes, I have two daughters, Louise and Melanie... they turned up today for a week, they didn't tell me they were coming, they're a bit like that... I should have told you before. I'm 55 years old. I've got this far... and I have two daughters. There... and I was married to their mother... once upon a time."

"I know how old you are… you don't have to remind me!' Nina was impatient and touchy. Quickly she felt the strange jab of jealously. "I thought since you'd been sharing so much of your life with me you might have said. Is your… is your ex-wife here as well?"

"No, she's not here," he said huffing.

"Melanie's twenty-two and Louise is twenty… Nina, please don't be cross… you're right, I should have told you… it doesn't affect the way I feel about *you*."

"Oh right, and how do you feel about me, exactly?" she realised this was a big, angry question but she was hot and propelled by bits of rage she couldn't conceal. She knew she was being irrational, but he *had* been wrong to keep it from her.

"I love you… very much," he said, gently and effortlessly. Why it was the most natural thing in the world to exclaim! Elegantly and keenly, the words seemed to double their effect.

"I'll write to you from Florence, and will come and see as much of you as I can… if you'll allow it."

She wanted to say 'I love you' in return and he wanted to hear it. She held back, viewing Arthur with an unexpected perspicacity. It made sense; a natural, obvious addition to his life. Of course, he would have daughters. It was just a surprise. She loved and cared for him and this is who he was and how he came. She placed her hands back inside his, perhaps the gesture would be a token of her love until she could confidently find the words. Writing to each other would be perfect. Creating a relationship through words, composing what would become a collection of correspondence was the challenge and the love of poets and romantics alike. They'd make memories in their written thoughts. Their letters would hold as much value as time spent together; they would fill the gaps and long distances before meeting again.

The atmosphere between them began to soften. The peaceful, tender-cream surroundings, the sage and aged artworks all seemed to breathe affectionately, aspiring to love: Cupid, Psyche, Eros, Anima, in whatever guise they appeared. Arthur and Nina had a new future ahead of them. It was both a continuation of Florence and something fresh. Nina, facing the hotel entrance, spied an urgent Aunt Merry, walking along the hallway. What could Nina read from her frowns and wrinkled brow. She was more concerned with staying close to Arthur and she didn't feel embarrassed. Nothing could stop a pressing Aunt Merry, steam-rolling down the carpet, having too many things to think about and all at the same time.

"Nina... hello dear... pardon the intrusion," she said turning to Arthur with a friendly, unjudging face, she'd reserve her opinions for later. "Nina, we had a phone-call to say the taxi's come... the flight's not at *four pm,* it's *fourteen hundred hours...* i.e. two o'clock... suffice to say *we have to leave now!*" She shook her head, "excuse me, but I must say it... but why, oh why the Italians have to use the twenty-four-hour clock is beyond me! And... um... it's all got lost in translation. I'll see you upstairs in a few minutes... if we are to catch this flight home we must hurry!" Aunt Merry, glad to expel her current exasperating news, smiled at Arthur and in a whole new voice she said sweetly, "you must come and visit us in Sussex." She agreed with herself, "yes, it's very quiet, reserved little town, a great change from your bustling, artistic city." She paused, looking about the interior, "I'm sure I will return here... I rarely say I *wouldn't return* to anywhere... but Florence is the *most* special place."

"Yes," said Arthur rising, "you are right... and I hope you *will* return. You must be Aunt Merry... I'm Arthur." They shook hands.

"Well of course you are... Hello my dear... now I shan't get in the way of the two of you, the spirits are telling me to hurry along!" Aunt Merry turned on her heels. She cried from the lift, "Nina, we must go very soon." Nina thought how her aunt had assumed so surely that she, Nina, would follow her and not choose to stay with Arthur. Nina had most definitely altered but not in the radical ways of feminists past; these times had changed, and there was no cause to be such.

In the quiet corridor, watched and blessed by ancient sculptures, icons and symbolic landscape paintings, nothing else could be said except a kiss goodbye.

When Nina and her aunt left the hotel the chaise longue cushion still held an imprint of Arthur, not one thing wished to forget him, even the Venus pudica statue looked mournful. Nina's once feeling of strangeness and odd emptiness was replaced with a love that was becoming deeper and wider; her happiness ready to be accentuated by a portfolio of letters, poems, of distant thinking and yearning.

When Nina finally came to opening her package containing the red handkerchief of Simon's and Arthur's address at Via di Fazzoletti, it was a clear, dark night at home in her bedroom. She had not unpacked her suitcase but her room felt both comfortable and cluttered. Inside the envelope she spotted a third item: a small, silk lady's handkerchief. The main body of the handkerchief was a damask rose pink with hand-painted deep red and pale gold roses flecked with white brushstrokes for detail. The free-pattern of roses were contained within a complementing pink-painted border, in line with the square shape of the handkerchief; a delicate white stitching completed the design. It was refined and unfussy and beautiful to hold, Besides Simon's red handkerchief, it was elegant and feminine and new. It had the pastel colouring of Rococo but not its extravagant exuberance. Arthur wrote, *'designed by Arthur Feilding for Nina Hurst. This is the first sample of a new range of handkerchiefs I am putting together, I'm calling it 'Nina'. This time a handkerchief with a reminder of my love: strong and constant.'*

Part XII

The Heinegette Handkerchief

In the April of 1988, Arthur had arrived at Via di Fazzoletti one day after the Easter weekend celebrations. Liza was always very pleased to see him. In age she could be neither mother nor sister but she delivered the Italian qualities of both. Their contact was not regular during the new year winter months. She always imagined him (and she was right) to be preoccupied with London life, his daughters and commitments to the family business in whatever shape or form. Simon was not a communicator so any source of news would derive from Arthur, the orator.

Liza was eager to start up the shop, hear his stories and encourage his new season ideas. Religious festivities over, the release of spring decorated Via di Fazzoletti in its traditional magic and the street once again became industrious and dusty, productive and alive. The little street's shop-houses and workshops would begin to trade again, uncertain how their future lay, year on year.

At the shop, Liza was responsible for letters and deliveries during the quiet period when both brothers were absent. In the studio, below stairs, there was a slender corner-desk where fragile parcels were placed, with a stamp indicating when they were received and who received them; letters and slim articles were filed in the short pigeon-hole structure above. It was always Liza who collected the post. If she was unwell, which she claimed never to be, her younger sister, who also worked in the studio, would help her.

Arthur was especially pleased to be back at home in Florence, and just as he had anticipated, a parcel from London had been waiting for him since February.

Arthur had spoken to Simon in the January just gone.

Sometime, before the turn of the year, Arthur had been aware of an up-and-coming, particularly unusual sale in London. How did he know? He moved in artistic circles. He was meticulous with his research. He had panache and verve, spiriting from the most reliable people, first-hand facts, knowledge and advice that would put him ahead, keep him prepared. He would say it was easy because, essentially, people like to tell you things (but you had to have a certain talent to extract information). In the appropriate circumstances, amongst those of a respectable group, it gives them elevation; with the right approach and encouragement, much might be revealed. Rarely did people hold back when talking to Arthur. He mixed with a great many experts and specialists in all fields of art, and although they thought themselves discreet, they seldom were, especially after two deep glasses of merlot:

'It's really a jumble-sale of war memorabilia, personal trinkets, ceramics, papers. They've been stored away in country houses since 1945. Can't say we'll see anything we haven't seen before. Might be worth going along to… Ducks is an attractive place… and while they prepare themselves for a big auction in the Summer, this small-scale one is a simple distraction; one to make-up the yearly numbers. They get fewer buyers in the winter… if it rains, even fewer. But that's the market…'

Arthur thought about his annual search, and the disappointment of so many sales, but he would never give up, he wouldn't allow defeat to lie on his shoulders. When would the tide turn in his favour? When it came to something as unassuming as a handkerchief, Arthur was a master, a connoisseur. He was eloquent and sophisticated and used these talents to his advantage, for the sake, as he believed, of the integrity and historical continuation of his family's handkerchief workshop, his business. For now, its success and development and the sacredness of its past depended on him, as well as Simon and their different abilities. As a gentleman and a buyer, each year Arthur would inquire at auction houses, antique shops, and many of London's high-end art rooms in his search. Where Arthur had words and artistry, Simon worked well under instruction; the heart-pounding, the nerve-shaking, the riskier, the better; the adrenaline was empowering. He could bring in the prize Arthur had set up: which, this year, he did.

With an unsteady hand, Arthur opened the parcel, a note inside read, 'Got it! Simon. Speak in April.' That was it, that was all. They did speak, two days after Arthur had opened the parcel (and not before) confirming its arrival and, most importantly verifying its authenticity. In the light of time passing peacefully, the buying event had become a snippet of history. Both men bided their time, Simon keeping low, out of range, travelling to a little town in middle Perthshire he had once seen on a postcard. Arthur had waited patiently to hear from Simon: had he bought the handkerchief? Simon was a man of minimal words; Arthur knew this from years of experience. He found the best way to extract any sort of relevant information from his brother was to ask questions, the right questions and hope for more. It was an excellent method, but he'd waited. He waited until he'd reached Florence.

Carefully folded inside, Arthur took sight of their prize, 'an Italian dark-green, silk handkerchief,' Lot 32, page 77 as stated in Ducks' catalogue.

Then in May the two brothers had spoken once more, an unscheduled call. Arthur had managed to track down Simon, thanks to Liza's list of ideas of places he might be. This time it was because Nina had significantly entered his life and revealed Simon's red handkerchief. More had been added to his elaborate escapade.

Arthur cleared the table of dust and debris, wiping the surface with a nearby cotton cloth. With the dry tips of his fingers, he lay the handkerchief on a velvet cloth he kept stored in one of the drawers. In poor light, below the table he fumbled for his special close-up lamp, plugged it in, it didn't work. He replaced the bulb with one he'd seen rolling around in the drawer and began again. Natural light, of which Florence had plenty, was perfect for an overall effect; close scrutiny of a handkerchief was better achieved in a dark room with an intense light.

He sighed and a chill ran down his spine. He shivered; his shoulders shuddered. He sobbed. Suddenly it was 1943. There was a jerk of confusion and the anguish and the alert intelligence of his 11-year-old self covered his senses. He could hear the cry of Signora Heinegette and, beyond the pained and feared look in her eye, he saw resolution.

The Heinegette family were silver-smiths. They had lived and worked at the far end corner of Via di Fazzoletti toward the Ponte Vecchio. It was said their ancestry could be linked to Benevenuto Cellini, the great Florentine Mannerist goldsmith. Certainly, they were a proud, hardworking family yet modest and kind and inclusive like all the good people on Via di Fazzoletti. Arthur's mother and her brother Piero were very friendly with the Heinegettes. There was always a strong understanding between the two men, Piero and Signor Heinegette; they held the same convictions and strong convictions were as powerful as a religious belief. Most nights, late, and as dark as a Mediterranean summer evening could be, when Arthur was semi-asleep and gazing at the moon and keeping cool from the summer heat, the two men would spend time in Piero's studio. In the morning, the candles would be drained, Uncle Piero always looked very tired and distant and Signor Heinegette looked pale and strained.

During the long school holidays Arthur would visit their busy silver-smiths shop. It was the coolest and shadiest position in the street, where a breeze, lifted from the Arno, seemed to curl round and through, into their front door. Every Friday Signora Heinegette used to bake a sweet, twisted loaf almost as colourful as the sunflower-yellow fields of Tuscany. Arthur used to watch her thump the dough and plait it roughly like a horse's tail. Later she'd keep back a piece for him. It had a soft crust and a generous crumb, and being a questioning, inquisitive boy he used ask how she made it. Why, in his long life (he was only eight and this made Signora Heinegette laugh) had he never tasted anything like it. She used to say she took a drop of hot golden butter from the sun just before it set on Thursday night; this was the secret ingredient and he was not to tell a soul. Arthur, as always, kept his word, and because she had shared such a valuable mystery, he not once questioned how she achieved it.

One early autumn day in 1943 a loud commotion hit Via di Fazzoletti; a street normally humming with activity and daily routine: blinds being extended, doors being unlocked and shutters being clanked and secured. This fated day was broken by a heavy, aggressive din. Shouts and screams and cries, high enough to reach the gods in heaven, were heard. In response the air was belted with attack, and offence and fury. A few minutes later, compelled by some unruly force, Arthur ran in the direction of the Heinegettes, where fierce sounds reverberated. He staggered and stopped beside a lamppost. He saw invasion. The Heinegette shop was being plundered by German soldiers. Shaking, Arthur watched, quickly hiding behind a pile of rubbish and old timber. Frightened and hypnotised, something tugged at him to stay, his eyes transfixed and his feet grounded. Bedraggled and terrified, Old Signor Heinegette, his son (Uncle Piero's friend), kind Signora Heinegette, and her two girls were rounded up and pushed toward the van. It all happened so quickly and violently.

Signora Heinegette tried to dab her eyes and then coughed and covered her mouth with one of Piero's handkerchiefs, this Arthur recognised. Their eyes locked, she had spotted little Arthur, and huddling her children as close as she could, cried out, turned briefly to him with that unforgettable stare and tossed her handkerchief to the ground. The Heinegette family were shoved aggressively into the machine; the spoils of their home were seized. The door slammed shut, loud enough to break glass and send a sharp shock through Arthur. Away they went, the van driven with anger and contempt, grinding its thick wheels, savagely eating its way through the streets. The hysteria, the thunder and the lightening of the scene which had arrived at great speed now ceased. Like the last clinging breath before death, an eerie silence deafened the street, and a painful reality spread over the earth. Arthur stood paralysed by a trickling chill. Within half an hour he returned home to his desperate mother and was, for the first and only time in his life, lost for words. He pulled from his pocket the handkerchief, thrown to him by Signora Heinegette, he was sure she had meant it for him. Uncle Piero and Arthur's mother exchanged meaningful glances and then spoke in an old, very fast Italian poor Arthur could not comprehend. He felt he didn't understand anything anymore; life was a mystery to him; the way people were thinking, what they were doing, it was senseless.

Via di Fazzoletti stayed silent, no-one opened their shops.

By the late afternoon Arthur's mother took him out, boarding the bus for Fiesole. Simon was six and was being cared for by Liza, who loved children. There was a very important job to do, no more time could be wasted; time was not thought of in days, it was thought of in minutes, hours. At his mother's request and pride, Arthur was now involved. She had tried to explain the current situation to him and to comfort him but he didn't listen, all he could see was Signora Heinegette's last look and the green handkerchief falling to the ground in one great, final, desperate gesture. Arthur would know what to do, Signora Heinegette had put faith in him.

His mother packed a small picnic, and dressed well.

Arthur was still distraught and confused; it seemed she was play-acting, putting on a happy face but underneath it all, a great drama was being cast.

The bus was very slow and hot. The passengers looked heat-stunned and wary. Arthur and his mother arrived at the stop before the Roman Theatre and walked a good three miles of rural pathways to their destination. They unpacked their picnic. Arthur wasn't hungry, all he could taste was gritty dust and grass pollens. They sat at the base of the amphitheatre fiddling with weeds and grass-tufts growing between the cold, ancient stone-steps. Arthur's mother ate nervously; pigeons cooed in the Cypress trees and the air was ironically fresh and liberating. Looking all about her, she reached inside her handbag and opened an envelope, inside lay Signora Heinegette's handkerchief. Today it would leave their safe hands and begin its journey; it would gather many scars and creases along the way and a new map would be imprinted on its future. This spot in Fiesole, The Roman Theatre and a rough meeting time had been, somehow, previously agreed. While they waited for its collection, Arthur's mother felt obliged to tell him of its vital significance (another secret he was bound to). So she did, and Arthur grew up and into the world much faster than was intended for his young age.

The Heinegettes, like Arthur's family, were members of a secret Italian underground society, fighting for an Italy free of fascism and dictatorship and invasion; the perilous situation they found themselves living in. They worked with Uncle Piero in the compilation of codes and cyphers and, when the time came for distribution, they used their contacts to help in his terrifying journeys through Italy. The two families established the ways and means of communication and the networking of other underground groups on the understanding and ambition of reaching the allies in England. This handkerchief, The Heinegette handkerchief, with its scribbles and scrawls and specific designs told of the locations and contact details of six other Italian agents running secret groups of freedom loyalists across Italy; primed and ready to help the allies. The intention was to get this handkerchief into the highest hands so the allies were able to plan and build safe attacks, find aid and assistance in sabotage and consequently overthrow the enemy. Of course, his mother spoke carefully and gently to him. The magnitude of him saving the handkerchief was profound; a second copy was never made. Once the handkerchief was made and encrypted, it was important to get rid of it instantly. All Arthur could think about was being helpless to save Signora Heinegette. His mother tried to make him see that by saving the handkerchief, the Signora had entrusted him with the next important stage of its life. What a great service he would do her. Then, but not knowing exactly when, his mother promised to take Arthur and Simon on safe passage back to England to see their fathers. The heavy air of Florence was choked by terror and fear: entrenched by German occupation and monumental destruction. Arthur needed to be taught to talk again and to find comfort in books and poetry, a solace she could not provide.

Not long after these details had been relayed, a young woman and her daughter arrived with a picnic. Arthur felt uncomfortable and swollen by emotion; fed too many words he feared. There was an exchange of nods between the two women. Arthur walked with his mother, side by side. They approached the two picnickers, his mother with a look of surety and kindness. The pale, exhausted young woman commented on the weather and how she'd foraged for some mushrooms on the pathway. She kept her arms quite still, unusual for Italians and her daughter seemed static, motionless; had she been told not to speak and to move in a whisper? These were dark days for a passionate, expressive country and any signs of high ebullience would have been deemed suspicious. Arthur's mother handed her a long sandwich of two slices of crusty bread and the envelope containing the Heinegette handkerchief tucked inside. She nodded gratefully, took the prize and left. Women and children were excellent covers for passing on secret information; they were less conspicuous; the ruling authorities rarely suspected them. And so, therefore, it must be assumed the Heinegette handkerchief made its way through Northern Italy, journeying over mountains and rivers, passing from hand to hand through dangerous hostile land and climbing up through France before being transported to safety across the Channel.

The Heinegette Handkerchief can claim a

remarkable campaign. Each time its life was potentially compromised, it was overlooked by the enemy: a pretty handkerchief, that was all. However, it was understood by the allies to be a carefully coded weapon of Italian groups ready to rise. Important letters and documents were censored, unsafe or burnt; they could be falsified. The radio-waves were intercepted. Double-agents existed on both sides, espionage was probable, trust was a rare commodity.

Looking particularly elegant and precious in a time of savagery, and having somehow (in discussions) been favoured as an extremely vital source to comprehend, The Heinegette Handkerchief fell into exactly the right hands at exactly the right time. It came to the attention of a notable commander, Frank Nelson, co-founder of The Special Operations Executive. This British organisation built a team. It was a band of code-breakers and cryptic analysts confined to a grand country house and operated by counter-intelligence who received the Heinegette handkerchief. Here it was spread out on brown paper on an oak-table in the Map room and studied amidst maximum security. The brains of S.O.E. worked on its encryption and quickly made use of its contents. As the war changed and activities altered the handkerchief was continually referred to, questioned, re-questioned and re-assessed.

When the war ended, these grand houses were abandoned, even Churchill's underground cabinet war rooms were left. War recruits, operators, staff, all walked out of their work-building, their offices and never looked back. Their task was now to build the future, as the past aged. It was accepted that the Heinegette handkerchief was boxed up, tidied away, like many other miscellaneous items: typewriters, map-scrolls, ink-stands, all trapped and forgotten in some stuffy attic. When owners died and the time came for inheritances to be sorted, boxes resurfaced and eventually a sale took place: 'Mid-20th century decorative curiosities.'

So here stood the 55-year-old Arthur in the presence of that very Heinegette handkerchief. It had finally come home, back to where it had started as a symbol of a service to the nation of Italy and the allies. For Arthur the duty was to his mother, to his uncle and to Signora Heinegette, whose wise eyes gleamed back at him across the years, as green as the green-bruised silk.

Part XIII

The Present, 2018
Nina and Arthur's story, by Nina

On returning home from Florence I realised I had to make a change. The Italian city had been a revelation; how could I not feel inspired to make a difference to my life? I loved living with my mum and sister, but without a doubt, I was a new person. It would be too easy, even for a complicated person, to slip back into a regular life, into an average and ordinary system. I would not allow it. My recent adventures had sharpened me. They'd shape a new future, for what good were experiences if they did not alter you and shift your perspectives and give your future a different destination. I felt strong and confident enough to prove it and there was no better time. I moved out of the safe Sussex country and into London life, ready to seriously pursue my career as a writer. As soon as I could I wrote to Arthur telling him of my transformation into the city-living girl, warning him he may not like this new mould of woman.

With an inheritance I bought a shoe-box-sized flat (it was my own and that was important). For a while I was too tired to furnish it and when Aunt Merry came to visit in the first week, she off-loaded a number of odd pieces she, 'no-longer had use for.' She had come by taxi, as she always did, having befriended the driver to help her with some removals. I looked at her very keenly for most of the items were brand new, still wrapped in their department-store boxes. She took me out for a full tea once a month and talked at me constantly. I was always grateful to her for the trip to Florence and although it was me who'd found a new way, it was she who'd laid the important path.

Within three months, propelled with the ferociousness to succeed and to eat, I was writing for a magazine company. In the few hours I had to myself I began to write short novels and of course frequent letters to Arthur. There was always something to say, and when days were difficult, I would concentrate on something beautiful and infuse all my romantic powers into a 'Florentine' letter, happy to have created something special for someone who loved me.

By September of the same year we had met again in Florence, then he made *me* the excuse to leave the shop on Via di Fazzoletti to come to London and my small home where, at last, we could spend time together. Liza, Arthur's great confidante, was left totally in charge in Italy. She was full of admiration and deep understanding and claimed Arthur's spontaneity and illumination was an Italian gift. New handkerchief designs were put 'on-hold.' This was no catastrophe since Arthur had been over-creative with his sketches and the little studio had been inundated with work and a back catalogue of commissions.

I had my fears that London would not be the backdrop of love and romance and adventure that Florence had been. The city was tough but innovative; and yet, because we *wanted* to love one another, to make the magic of Florence and its early beginnings survive, our love was made greater and would have worked on any stage in the world. I believed in it and so did he. The more time I spent with Arthur on his visits to London, the richer my fictional narratives became with sub-plots and twists that attracted attention. In the first two years I visited Florence four times, each time in the six-month period Arthur studiously worked there. We returned on his motorbike to places that held such personal meanings: Villa Angelo in Fiesole, the Cemetery, the Arno and naturally much time was spent at Via di Fazzoletti, which rather sadly, over those two years, had seemed to evolve into a more touristic street.

By not living together and having the distance of different destinations between us, it somehow kept us more devoted and attached. Letters and poems, back and forth drew me close to his heart. I know how much he enjoyed writing; love inspired his poetry, an artform he admired but felt he couldn't emulate. My advice was poetry did not look to being perfect, it didn't hold peaks of perfection; it was just happy you had found pleasure in exploring its medium. We agreed words found in poetry flowed freely, almost subconsciously and, with each new reading, you could find more and more within them. Once written they were bound to the page, like paint to a canvas, a vision or a thought was formed and crafted and art was made. Poetry and handkerchiefs were codes awaiting encryption.

In London we visited many of the same haunts. Together or apart, when he returned to Florence, the little cafés, music clubs, caves and caverns, galleries and gardens became our memories. In the winter months, London was bustling and lively. There were work parties for me and several family gatherings. Aunt Merry gave us tickets to the theatre, and after Florence she began to travel on organised bus group tours, forfeiting foreign churches for English cathedrals. Arthur would attend auctions and private sales as usual. I would write most days. We talked about everything and shared stories, covering the years behind us. Arthur said once, the wait and the discovery of me had been like the wait and discovery of the Heinegettte handkerchief, it had been worth living his complicated life. Sometimes we'd just sit together and say nothing at all and let our minds race and our thoughts relax and not waste breath on fear and parting. Arguments were few; time did not allow the mind reasons to argue.

One sunny day, after staying with my mother in St Leonard's for a weekend, Arthur and I took an unforgettable motorbike ride. It was a spur-of-the-moment gesture, though an air of opportunity and bright sun and the free openness and independence that comes after kind hospitality certainly added to the idea. I wrote a brief description of it in my diary. It was a journey of natural magic and I had to capture it, just with a few key words, to make it stand out among other days as it had done in life.

We were bound for Beachy Head and beyond. Arthur believed it was the bike making the discovery, choosing the paths and the turns. The sky was a creamy blue with a scattering of plump clouds like sailboats at sea and known to me as East Sussex sailors. Climbing the coast-road from Eastbourne, we were directed to the cliff-edge and over the Sussex Downs. Looking in all directions and holding tight to Arthur, layer after layer of rolling fields and woods opened before us. Chocolate-coloured cows and straying ponies and grazing sheep were dotted about the landscape like little staged figurines. The air tasted of dry straw or turned soil. We stopped at Birling Gap for a rest and for the vista. It was low tide on the beach. People were throwing stones in the sea as it lapped its salty-churned waves onto the receding shoreline. Bare-footed shell-pickers strolled on the wet patches of gritty sand. Little children with nets and buckets gathered around the many rock-pools teasing each other with long strands of purple and green seaweeds.

We rode on through the flint-stone villages with their cricket pitches and picket fences and barns. From a high road, descending gently down, we saw the sun shimmer on the ox-bow lake of Cuckmere Haven; a meandering stretch of water leading down to the sea. We were higher than the cries of seabirds. Here the air was even fresher, it was the freest air I had ever breathed, nothing had ever been spoken in it, like a clean sheet of paper we might write our love on. For we were the explorers, the adventurers and the seekers of beauty, of memories, and of tales to recall.

A little further around and on a high viewpoint, with the sun behind us, we marvelled at the distinctive curve of pure-white chalk and sharp, grey flint cliffs: The Seven Sisters. A magnificent sweep of land meeting sea made for the cartographer's fine pencil to sketch. The dramatic scenery and the joy of the adventure gave Arthur the impulse to kiss me. "I can't believe, at my age, I've been lucky enough to find *you*… a love like ours comes but once in any lifetime."

After making our way west along the coast we turned inwards to Pevensey, choosing a narrow, unmarked road, winding like the back of a snake along the Levels. The water dykes ran parallel to the road. We startled waders and birds of prey in our wake. We met no-one for over an hour. Just us. We'd left the whole world behind. It was like being awake in a dream: sunshine, a warm seasonal breeze and uninterrupted scopes. I hugged Arthur. One day, in my mind, the memory of all this would take me back to him and conjure the joy I felt.

Not long after this adventure and two years into our affair, Nib was born. Conceived, perhaps, out of many nights and mornings of intense loving; passion, nakedness and directness, no inhibition but a shared sensual ambition. Desire and want are empowering emotions. In body and soul I felt him possess me and yet I always owned myself, stronger and more empowered with his affection. Spirit overtaking sense and all senses overtaken, there was a calmness and a wildness; an animal energy, a human power, a god-like greed to please and fill the hours. Our love composed something anew and safely gave us Nib.

At first, Arthur's two daughters Louise and Melanie were doting, gentle and kind. Then on seeing a little brother arrive and grow with great affection, they promptly went off to start families of their own. Knowing how preoccupying and exhausting motherhood was and how it whisks you into a world dependent on nearby support, I saw very little of them. Both had married Italian men and taken Italy as a home. My sister and mother helped enormously and Aunt Merry bought so many teddy-bears, I considered moving to a larger flat. Our small flat had direct-access via a spiral staircase to a communal garden of three green acres with large plane trees, cherry blossoms, a centre garden of shrubs and bushes, and a play-area for all ages. At last we could make full use of all its freshness. I didn't want to move away from this urban-rural idyll. There was no possibility of extending what we had, so when there was a whisper the floor above may soon be available, Arthur offered to purchase it before it reached the open-market; it was a good investment. For us, the extra space and light were ideal and I hoped it would encourage Arthur to stay longer but he was too bound by the routine in himself and always stayed the same length of time. He was a relaxed and easy father to a son who equally adored him, yet each time he left us to return to Florence to fulfil a duty he could not delegate, it was very painful. Nib grew to understand how his father operated; it meant I had to deal with Nib's lowness, and the dark days, while Arthur remained the distant, elusive and exciting father taking part in all the good times. Nib's illnesses and long-nights of upset and his incidences at school became my sole responsibility. For a single parent, day and night, it became very weakening, even with some help. Gradually I grew contentious which, I gathered, was exactly what had happened to Arthur's ex-wife. I was falling into the trap of becoming the person I didn't want to be and quickly I had to put an end to this rising characteristic, which in its turn, would pick up conflict and even jealousy. I did not want it to engulf me; to become bitter and belligerent. I had seen women turn ugly and disagreeable in nature, stuck inside relationships, trying to alter the man they had married. This is why we never married, neither of us were the type and it seemed we would maintain a better relationship by being independent of each other. Arthur would make gestures, like buying the flat above, and other kind and spontaneous moves. Somehow by not being locked into a contract (we were both too free-spirited for that), it made our love closer. Arthur was older and had been through the struggles and difficulties of marriage. He did not seem to change his ways for anyone, although, perhaps *he* would say he did.

Arthur created a baby-blue silk handkerchief in honour of Nib, who was christened Robert. Robert would nibble the handkerchief with his sore baby gums and thus the name 'Nib' stuck. He was also very fond of pens so it seemed doubly appropriate to call him Nib. No-one called him Robert, it was a stand-by, grown-up name. I took Nib out to Via di Fazzoletti many times and Liza loved to entertain him in her Italian-nonna way. Nib's first word was 'nonna' which delighted Liza who couldn't help but tell the whole street in her radiant and flamboyant fashion. At each step Nib grew to stand-out amongst his peers. He was as beguiling, charming and captivating as his father, this I know, and as deep and thoughtful as his mother, so I'm told.

It was easy to feel lonely without Arthur and yet at the same time he was already there, if not in person, then in the spirit of a place. Perhaps I should be glad that I was able to imagine him everywhere, for his early sudden death was such a striking blow. I was distraught and angry at the same time. For so long I imagined him out in Florence, wandering, riding, working, biding his time before coming back to me in London. I'd wait for a letter or parcel to fall through the letterbox as they had done so over twelve long loving years.

Arthur died peacefully at his studio desk, his side-light shining directly over an unfinished handkerchief. Unable to handle such grief, Liza contacted Simon who came and with the help of Louise, fastidiously cleared and re-arranged the shop. Arthur's belongings were gathered and dispersed, according to his wishes. His ashes were sacrificed to the green fields of Tuscany. Prayers were said at Santa Trinita church. Liza retired; Simon wrote a brief note to me with an Italian scrawl from Liza. Simon later disappeared. I never returned. This was the one place, the shop on Via di Fazzoletti, I could visualise him, standing tall and dominant at the open door, his shiny motorbike nearby, ready for an impromptu excursion.

A further three months passed and the Via di Fazzoletti shop and studio, no-longer had the heart, the aspirations or the will to continue. Arthur had been its blood and air, so its life was over too. I kept on with my writing but spent long hours staring into space: a fathomless void. Each day I cried a little, watching flickers of Arthur in Nib, as he grew and talked and tried to be brave and obedient, desperately wanting to rebel, but always behaving well as if told to do so by an older figure. He wanted to be told off by his father, to learn by his example, to make him love him when he fell or failed and to make him proud when he strove to succeed. Tears were not a remedy but they were a release. In our own way Nib and I grew, week on week, and the past stepped further and further back, into its age.

Part XIV

The Present, 2018 - Nib returns home

In the mild September sunshine, Nina busied herself with the terracotta pots on the front patio and windowsill. She untangled the orange and purple pansies and cut back the tired brown geranium heads; they had been a vibrant, elegant coral-red all spring and summer. She re-tied her Spanish jasmine to its wooden trellis and encouraged the young wisteria to twirl away from the front door. A little tidying up and brushing away of leaves and displaced soil after days of strong winds and heavy downpours was a satisfying task. She felt in control once more. Peace had resumed and she could get out and bring about neatness and order relatively quickly.

It was two weeks since Nib's letter had arrived and in that time she had gracefully and honestly written about Arthur, their time together and something of herself. When she'd felt a surge of sadness or regret, she was spurred on by the desperate plea of Nib's voice, like that of a small boy, willing her on. Secretly she had been glad the rain had come. It had kept her mostly indoors and focused, and although she did not like to feel trapped by weather, she felt compelled to complete her writing. She had done what she considered her best, but there was no best or better, right or wrong. Her stories were recollections and reflections, recalled by her mind and her eye. It was something for Nib to hold and own. Perhaps it might help him to move on with his life, to not hold back, to make something of himself and not feel he was always searching for his father's side. So many of Arthur's qualities he instinctively possessed. Nina could see them and would tell Nib so. It pleased him to hear it, but it was not enough. He was always questioning, seeking answers, and looking for Arthur. He wanted to have something to hold.

Nina had placed her mug of tea on the wide arm of her garden chair. She placed a ginger-nut beside it, thinking she would be only a few minutes. As a gardener she should have known this was not the case. Twenty minutes had lapsed before she'd considered taking a sip; for time spent pottering outside moved at a different rate to time indoors, which was methodical, registered by quarterly chimes or radio pips. The tea was cold and the biscuit had been found by a family of ants who after a few bites were ready to lift the entire specimen and magic it away to their spice-loving colony.

Gathering her garden clippers, a bag of leaves and the handle of her mug, Nina went inside and closed the door. Within a minute there was a long rat-a-tat-tat, her heart fluttered, he must have been watching her. On the door-step stood Nib.

"Oh Nib, you're…" she tried to compose herself, but she was a mother full of emotion and she just couldn't and wouldn't, not for her lonely, wandering son.

"I'm home… yes!" He dropped his suitcase and gave her a big hug. Something they had both needed for a long time and more than she'd realised.

He was looking weary and thinner and she told him so.

"I'm sure you'll see to that…" he said. He seemed impatient Nina thought and she knew why. When you come home you want to do everything at once; a drink, a snack, a wash, unpack and change. Nib needed to do all that, but most of all he wanted to settle on the stories of his father.

"Did you get my letter?" Nib rubbed the tabby cat's ear and sat down beside him, his head down and distracted. "I was feeling a bit down…"

"Yes, and I've put something together for you, a booklet… well, a file… a record of memories," said Nina, smiling. Nib brightened.

"I'll get us something to eat, then later we'll go to the storage hut. There are some containers in there I've not touched for years… I don't even know what's in some of them… and now you're here, we can go through them together." This seemed to Nina like a perfect bonding project, to get Nib talking and thinking again and resolving some of the insecurities in his mind.

"Ok, sounds good," Nib said placidly. He was so tired; he would have agreed to anything. Nina fetched some soda-bread she'd made. Her mother had written out an old Irish recipe for soda-bread on a still-life postcard from the National Gallery and Aunt Merry had done the same on headed paper from Fortnums; their writing was very similar. For years they had found another bone of contention to squabble over: which had the better recipe, by method and ingredients. It was Nina who discovered they were exactly the same, and from the same source; so she kept the two side by side. After a thick slice of bread, butter and fig jam, Nib still maintained his continental tastes, he fell asleep: a dozy, woozy disorientated sleep. He was awoken by the cat licking his fingers, then it tootled out through the open window, no-longer interested in being stroked.

All the while, the early afternoon held its backdrop of deep, deep-blue sky and fresh spiderwebs had been spun between scaly orange, Chinese lanterns. Nina had laid out her organised file on the sitting-room table, full of the writings she had made at Nib's request. She called it simply, 'For Nib.' She'd left it for him to pick up. Nina had been out checking her garden pots, she couldn't help fiddling with them. She was nervous. When she'd finally come inside, the file had gone and a cup of tea was in its spot.

Nina's storage hut was formerly a bike and paint-brush shed. It was not attached to the cottage but located outside the back-door where there was also a round flower-bed and grasses. She had paid a reasonable sum for an intensive damp-proof course, making it entirely dry and mould-free. Nina had downsized her life many times over but very specific, unopened, boxed possessions had always travelled with her. Inside these were Arthur's belongings. By keeping them sealed and semi-detached from her cottage life Nina kept the memory of Arthur in another room, one she seldom entered. His possessions were preserved and she thought, if she opened them up, everything might disintegrate or dissolve. This thought of ruination she had believed too sincerely. It was her way of dealing with loss, by keeping the past tucked away, knowing it was all there; conserved for when she needed it, but never actually approaching it. Really, she had kept it hidden and enclosed. She didn't want to re-live her sadness and loss. She didn't want Nib to be unhappy or see her unhappy. All the time she had been trying to protect them and yet this was exactly what would make him happy. They would open the boxes and learn, laugh and cry and celebrate Arthur.

Nina unlocked the hut and she and Nib, in turn, took great care opening the chests, one at a time. They were high-quality, sturdy and lined. Very gradually they began to lightly investigate the items, sifting aside a few pieces. Several handkerchiefs came to the surface, some of the last to leave the shop on Via di Fazzoletti. There were Arthur's seasonal handkerchiefs from over the years, he had always held back one of each design, there was a large envelope of commissions paid for but never collected. Arthur had told Nina these incidences occurred, on average, three times a year. They found a tiny selection of Uncle Piero's handkerchiefs marked with the red lily, il timbro di giglio.

"Look Nib… Uncle Piero's handkerchiefs made from 1947 to 1966…" Nina said pointing, "you'll read about that…" she paused and said softly, "it's unlikely we'll find a freedom handkerchief."

"Look here!" she cried lifting up a fragile silk handkerchief, "this damask pink handkerchief your dad named the Nina range… and here's the baby-blue one he created for you!" Nina turned away. This was just as hard as she thought it would be. She expected Nib to feel the same but he was entranced and excited by it all. It was a Christmas of memories for him. So with strength and a warm energy they ploughed on. Nib found a note from Uncle Piero, it was written in Italian and translated underneath by Arthur. He read it aloud:

'In memory of our alliance and the success of the S.O.E campaign during World War II, in November 1954 on the celebration of Winston Churchill's 80th birthday, I (Piero) sent the great man a dove-white handkerchief with my red lily mark. I am told he is often seen wearing it in his top pocket. I read this as a symbol of our secret solidarity.'

"Goodness… well, well… that family… your dad's family, always full of surprises… that I *didn't* know."

"You see mum," said Nib, "you're enjoying this

more than you thought you would." He wanted her to feel at ease, to be lifted, not burdened. It was difficult for Nina and Nib to match their feelings, but she tried to brighten with each unveiled box.

What happened next was unexpected and remarkable. It was Nib's finding, and rightly so, it should have been found by him; it *was* destined to be his. Perhaps an hour had passed, maybe two, for the time was theirs to fill. Nib looked down on an old, brown folded coat and again in Arthur's steady hand, whose handwriting never faltered, he read, *'For Nib, my son.'* In smaller writing beneath he read, *'Uncle Piero's winter coat... from the days of Monte Cassino.'* Nib was crouched down beside the chest, Nina put her hands on his shoulders and gasped. Nib handed the note to his mother and as he stood up, pulled out the coat to its full length, shook off the stale air and insult of dust.

"This was meant for me." He said in a non-begrudging tone. How could he be angry? He didn't bother with such a useless, negative, vacant emotion. It did not achieve anything except lock you into sorrow and gloom. Nib was attractive; it was loss that had wearied him. The coat had been forgotten, simple. What was important now was what it revealed.

"Uncle Piero's coat from the days of Monte Cassino," repeated Nina, listening very attentively to the words formed, as if they really meant something else. Another one of Arthur's encryptions. Yes, that was it!

"Nib!" she cried "look for the pockets... no, no the inner pockets."

"There aren't any!" He replied.

"Feel the inner lining then."

They lay the coat down as if attending a sleeping person, fully stretched out across the flat lids. Nina examined the stitching, perfectly neat and clean to the eye. Better than she could do, but then she'd not been faced with *this* trust. She softly ran her hand across the lining like Nib before her and then she smiled, broadly. She beamed. She tingled with goose-bumps; the anticipation was frightening and thrilling. She ran back to the cottage and to her sewing-machine. She picked out her finest scissors; the smallest pair with the sharpest point. Nib was slightly dazed. Then he watched his mother in fascination as she began to unpick the stitches one by one. He feebly protested but she ignored him. When she reached the final stitch she said,

"It was Liza who stitched all the freedom handkerchiefs into the lining!"

"So?" Nib wasn't sure she was really talking to him; he didn't understand her phrases. Was this another era in Italy he was always too young to remember?

"This stitching was done much later... I remember

now… I remember the action rather than anything that was said… I can see her gestures. Oh goodness… Nib!"

"What?" said Nib, slightly irritated. *"What is it?"* He was desperate to understand.

"I promise you this will all make sense very soon… oh I'm so glad to have written everything down for you… you were right to make me…" Nina turned her head and blew lightly on her hand to cool it down, "look!"

She slid her delicate hand inside the loosened lining. With a gentle tug she pulled out a green, slightly wounded silk handkerchief.

"Another handkerchief!" said Nib, "dad really did keep everything."

Nina looked directly at Nib; his eyes flashed the deep grey-green of Arthur's. He had grown taller than him, maybe another inch that afternoon. The revelation had given her tears to blink back at her beautiful son. She was rather shaky and managed to speak before the surprise caught her tongue and stunned her to silence, *"This is the Heinegette handkerchief!"*

Epilogue

Onwards and beyond,
as told by Julian (Giuliano)

The peculiarities of a modern family life are such that my mother is Arthur's daughter and Nib is Arthur's son (in Italian terms we are family).

Arriving in London, Nib had invited me along to his small house on a leafy green hill in Hampstead. The length of my stay was indefinite, like that of my own life before me I had time to waste and time to be idle and naive. I had few friends, a small allowance and was struggling with my unreliable roots as a travelling actor, and perhaps, he too had been this way once, we shared a similar strain. Nib was likeable and generous and after a bottle of decent Malbec, very talkative; after two bottles, loquacious and creative, drawing out his own melodies on a harmonica.

With his distinct style, unqualified chatter stuck to this man in look, but not in name (for it must be said that apart from the early loss of his father, no-one knew anything more intimate). The habitual townfolk saw nothing of Nib's depth and thought him a mysterious figure. Ironically, I found this internal, self-sufficiency made spectators think him aloof and vague. It's true he was very detached from the sociable community he lived in, but mostly his character and history were a confusion of whispers and gossip. When he did make the short, downhill walk from his home into the mainstream crowds, it somehow made his appearance all the more stirring. In doorways and on corner-stones, it was only natural people would want to talk about him; to have his name on their tongue, to spit a little rumour from their lips, to divulge more to their neighbour, to embroider a tale and refashion a story just to keep their mouths and ears well-dressed in the latest tittle-tattle nonsense.

It always felt such an honour to walk beside him, as if I'd attached myself to the first dazzling star of the evening. I had to scamper to catch up with him, his stride nearly twice as long as my own. He tended to wear a hat and, during the hot summer, his linen jacket would flap in the wind making him even wider and more impressive. Nib had the high forehead of intelligence and a tremendous trademark laugh which echoed around the house like a jungle bellow. Every day he listened to the radio, masterly copying the range of voices, keeping up to date with world news and yet, he lived in dated, messy surroundings, resembling a scene from back-stage theatre, exiting his front door to perform as his unusual self.

I remember one long summer's evening; the sky was a dark petunia purple. The bushy honeysuckles climbing up the doorway had split their pink curls; the invisible pollen with its sugary scent floated seductively yet lethargically in the still air; only the competitive bees were as drunk as I found myself.

Tiny thunder flies circled the over-ripe fruits and I seemed neglectful. Nib's faculties always appeared appropriate for the occasion, where I was an inebriated fool or ignorant youngster, he was successful in keeping his rationale in perfect tact. He had respectful eyes, he had seen many scenes in his life, and he did not judge. I had felt judged since I was born; my hair the wrong shade of brown, my left-handed writing hard to read. I was the one who bore second-place: the runner-up. Perhaps I came to acting simply to provide my straying self with characterful qualities I failed to own as myself. Nib was the first person I sincerely admired and the first time I understood what it meant to hold someone in high esteem. To me he was faultless because he had faults; this made him rich and fascinating. If I stood close, I longed to tease out some of his acuity and wisdom, but I never did, simply because in his presence you cannot help but stand back and observe him; even in my own life I felt like a side-lined second lead. As time progressed, I benefited from his advantages and sharpened up my own lackadaisical act, not to consider equalling him but to qualify as his respectful guest.

Nib had some tenuous memories of his father. Ten true years was all the life he could muster, with maybe five or six years of piecing together the sentimental, early childhood days. The memory was a strange mixing bowl of pictures and places.

In the early days Nib had seen his mother desperately upset, but she rallied with dignity for the sake of her son and of sense. He knew how madly in love they had been, and he hoped himself to one day find such love. He did not think himself a lucky man, fortunate in some ways but not lucky, and made me see the difference: 'luck is a force, it may befall you or it may not, fortune is something you carve yourself.'

Most days, Nib, in a concentrated and retrospective mood, shared with me something of his life and odd bits of his parents' life, sometimes repeating himself. It did him good to reminisce, to conjure his memories, hoping each time his father might live a little longer. Nib spoke each week with his mother. There were letters, written and read, but Nib believed it was important to talk on the phone. The voice betrays the soul by its tone, and the rise and fall of rhythm are the musical accompaniment to conversation. Where writing allowed for fore-thought, a phone exchange caught the spirit directly and settled their closeness. Since Nib's extensive travelling had come to a periodic rest, he met with his mother at her cottage once every couple of months and always came home enlightened. He built a cupboard for his curiosities, items I never caught sight of, and kept close a file of stories his mother had given him. These were Nib's untouchable treasures.

I spent five wonderful, youthful months with Nib. I grew up and grew out more than I had ever done. I worked in the local 'Stable-yard' theatre as both a set-coordinator and an understudy for an obscure play, taking to the stage five times when the third main-lead fell sick. During that time Nib would write, read and organise his thoughts and allow his mindfulness to come together. He had many artistic talents, a gift for words and a flair for fashion and they rewarded him with praise but paid him little money. Nib seemed to chip away at a healthy quarry of bank funds, using money casually and rarely replenishing his stocks. He played with his resource as if it was renewable, and this was his luxury. I was a saver, hoarding what I earned and benefitted from his infinite generosity; this did not extend to free lodging, for which I paid a small monthly rent. I had overheard his worth (my ears could not avoid it) was an accumulation of two substantial inheritances; riches and prosperity made for idle speculation. I was more ashamed to have eavesdropped on two low-degree locals than I was at questioning the eligibility of his business, as the business of their thoughts. As a beneficiary of his kindness I would not broach the delicate subject of money, especially if from its source stemmed many difficult narratives or worse, great sadness.

One, early morning, just like that, the season changed and the days following it felt cooler, sweeter and calmer. The leaves of the chestnut trees were browning, half-prickled conkers fell in cushioned thuds, little birds were twittering in the hawthorn bushes and the air tasted of smoked chocolate and cooked apples. It was a heady mix of flavours. My young, relaxed self was high on the fame of treading the boards for the fifth time, and a somewhat altered person having spent invaluable time with Nib. How wise and big and authoritative he always appeared and I told him so. He, himself, seemed changed that day and stunned me to another silence when he spoke. He spoke as if he had been planning these very words for years and had now found the moment for which they were meant:

"I've decided to take a trip to Florence... to Via di Fazzoletti... take care while I'm gone, I may well be sometime."

Via di Fazzoletti was a name I had heard from my mother yet despite having an Italian father, we had remained in England. I had not been anywhere close to my Italian heritage. It was Nib's turn to explore these tracks.

....

Nib filled his worn, brown-leather bag with a few items and strung the wide leather strap over his shoulder. Before departing his curious room, he took down a photograph from the mantelpiece and scrutinised the image. There stood his impeccably dressed father, a handkerchief in his top pocket; a man of great stature and solidity bending down to hug and love a small boy smiling his milky white teeth to the camera. He was pulling away slightly from the safe and tender embrace, his little body against his father's chest. His father looked so proud, gazing in awe at the little son he had made. Nib recalled the craggy, cliff-top in Cornwall, the pink clover clumps, the series of sharp rocks below, lashed and repeatedly worn by ferocious waves; they had looked like an alligator's spine. After a short stroll the salty sea-air had made him queasy but he'd promised himself he would not ruin his brown sandals, so he'd hid the sick rumblings at the pit of his stomach, sucking on a peppermint his mother had to hand. Still, he could not remember how they had ventured there, or where they had stayed. Not the slightest tug of the mind could bring about the whole circle of events leading up to the one snapped moment and, if he found the location and went to the same preserved spot again, the unchanged view of a seascape hundreds of thousands of years old, would be different from how he perceived it now, staring down at the dry photo in a hardy gold-brushed frame. From some household move it must have caught the damp, for there was a thin wrinkle running through the film, making the memory feel old but now less far away. Smiling, to keep a tear from falling, he slipped the photo carefully into his bag and took it with him.

THE END

Poems

After All

Last Evening

Temporary

What I Have Now

A short story

The Theatre on Latimer Street

After All

Sometimes,

More often than not and

More times as I learn

I am as I am:

Enough.

I look to myself, to whom

I was never really introduced

And see there, somewhere, smiles.

Hidden delight

Interspersed with reflections of woe.

From the bows, I took

To the pains, mayhem and madness,

I strived too much; was it worth the gains?

I never lessened;

I Softened.

And now, surrounded by those I love

Loneliness and uncertainties disperse.

Doubt, disbeliefs once intricately bound,

My round, mirrored tears dry up.

With time, the interludes of calm extend
And give back beauty to the friend

That is you

For sometimes, more often than not, I say

I am as I am:

Enough.

Last Evening

Last evening, the hours swept through the night

As if brushed by time into another's life.

I felt very distant from you,

I never wanted to be, so much

Did I crave a space to be close

And hide away awhile with only our speaking eyes

Seeking more than shallow voices.

Not even my long shadow could touch your hair

That I might feel something of you.

Not even the breeze of my spirit could chase your scent

That I might taste something of you

Or take sail round your soul for an invisible embrace.

And then the night was over.

For weeks I re-lived every part of it

Finding new ways for us to come together.

In some orchestrated action of surprise

In some subtle unexpected drift, whereby

I take your hands, as they fall to me

They form my deep remembered dreams.

I know I heard the earth sigh in the silence

And tremor and murmur at the brilliance of stars.

Then the day grew

I was covered again by long-lit hours

And all my thoughts of us

Lie harboured in a dark bed.

Temporary

I am mindful of the temporary

Passing of emotions

The minutes of the first and last

Coming of commotion

And all the days of loveliness

At the realisation of devotion

Dissolve into a pocketful of pretty little pasts

The memories sitting stained and wet on shafts of grass.

Time has played a skilful role

In which you sailed away

Nothing is ever permanent

Everything will swerve, will sway – and today

Displays another of these futures placed apart

The distance of horizons and the calling of my heart.

What I Have Now

What I see now, I have seen before
Once in a room of white
Whether it was by the day restored
Or dark in a shrouded night
The mind has many a thousand flaws
And harbours their mysteries deep
To make its mistress more the fool
Teased by the pleasantries of sleep

What I feel now, I have felt before
Once on a soft-pillowed bed
Knocking in rapture upon a white door
Kissing my eyes as he fled
But my mind is hazy in all that it stores
The stories are awkwardly read
They ebb and flow, back and forth
Like tidal waves pulled in my head

What I have now, I have had before
As the spring bird swallows his tune
So keen to rejoice on its' green-filled shore
Far from the desert's dune.
Thus I'm united with all that I know
And all that I know is this
Where I am going, who I so love
They have come to me all before
Mingling and merging the dreams into life
And somewhere we'll meet once more

The Theatre on Latimer Street

I had been three months in southern France when the phone rang. I could tell, before seeing the long number, it was an English caller; there was a polite persistence about the ringing tone. Someone hurried me, and, at the same time, apologised profusely for an untimely disturbance. If I chose to ignore the immediacy of the phone, a brief, perfunctory message would be recited, and, at my own convenience, I might respond. Of course I would answer. The last few weeks, à la francaise, had been as dull as ditch-water. At last someone needed me, they wanted to bother me, and interfere with my time, and in doing so conjured the thrill of anticipation an unplanned call always used to do. It was as if my blood came alive again, having been left to bake and boil and turn me into a sluggish sloth, it now raced around my body and sparked the parts I feared had died from timeless boredom.

To be honest I was finding the whole 'azure-coast relaxation' rather tedious. I suspect it had to be a mixture of my tastes and persona alongside the tempo and the people. I had thought it a reliable, do-able, achievable sort of indulgent section of France, resting on its eras of history like heavy books on an old bookshelf. I would move from celebrated old town to old town before I'd been in each too long. Reading too deep into the current stories and jostling too close to the gossip that follows, I feared becoming part of the funny fabric of its salubrious and ostentatious past. I wanted to leave no trace of my ever having stepped a foot on the wide promenade or tanned on the seafront or a toe dipped into the sea. Thus, when I felt I was close and fast-sinking into a familiar society that implores to know your name and from that one word master your business; that shakes its purse for attention, the irresistible, seasonal sound of paying notes between thumbs, I would depart. Traceless, nameless and gone. Taking a caterpillar train, curving along the sheer cliff edge, eating into the granite rock, I'd find another town and another indulgent group, making love to the November sun and thinking themselves quite clever. The only muddy darkness they would encounter would be a morning coffee, the only cause of complaint would be an ache from tennis or a numbness from swimming, a cough from too many smokes on the veranda. All might be remedied with a reminder of a drinks party, a golfing luncheon or the current arrival of a new wave of English. The Englishman to whom arrows of questions would be fired, their answers spread, accurately or inaccurately around the group, select or non-select. For everyone fed on everyone else's news long before tomorrow's gazette was dry, rolled and hanging in a linen-cloth bag on the handle of your door.

Therefore, the persistent ringing tone of the phone, the English caller, was a lifesaving bell to my bored self. I wanted to feel important again. Hell! I was a retired thirty-year old, single, ex-city banker.

I'd made enough money for one comfortable life; kept an expensive square, grey flat in London with an orchid on the round, glass table and perfectly fluffed rectangular, crisp pillows. Wealthy people feel in control if their empty domestic worlds are designed by shapes.

This journey to France was my recuperation period after five years in an ambitious money-making race. From the five of us city boys that made a good sum, I was the least messed up. James had returned home to his parents with two pages of prescription drugs; Will had married his long-term girlfriend, in the hope of embracing a new, quiet life and purposely locking himself out of his old one. John was in therapy after collapsing under the pressure of giving over every waking and sleeping hour to the fierce and furious task of making money as quickly as you made blood. At a cost to his soul and to his pocket, he used the money earnt to make his destructible, burnt-out self better again. Bobby was dead. He'd fallen from a second-floor balcony at a Holland Park club-party. He wanted to go, instantly and inebriated.

Our twenties had expired. I moved into the third decade of life worn down, worn out and looking for respite in a place to respire. Sadly, Southern France offered no inspiration. I suffered the life of repetition and boredom, both set fast like a sticky glue until I feared I might never escape from an atmosphere that became more stifling the longer you lingered. Yet now, someone had called me: a call to bring me back home. The sea-air, the pine-cone oils, the salty spray, the long rays of sun, their time was over. They had worked a freshness on my face, cleaned my lungs and cleared the mind of a brutal hardness. As a hangover from those arrogant twenties I remained doggedly judgemental and formed critical, and to my mind, logical analyses about everyone and everything I encountered.

The man on the phone I thought to be an old teacher of mine: a clipped, matter-of-fact, light voice.

'Henry Simmons?'

'Yes, that's me, who's this?'

'I'm David Smyth. I'm a solicitor at Smyth and Sons of Spitalfields... your great-aunt's solicitor of forty years.'

'My great-aunt?' We were a small family; relations of mine rarely cropped up. The living ones had given up at least five years ago, so thinking, in reaction to that thought alone, someone must have died.

'Yes, your great-aunt, Anne Munroe.'

'Oh my... my aunt Annie, yes.' I paused, the connection was not reliably clear so I decided to put the dear, delicate man out of his misery and difficulty before he, supposedly, put me into my mine, 'your ringing to tell me she's dead?'

'Yes, I'm afraid so. Yesterday, it was very quick. I heard you were in France.' Clearly it was easier to get solicitors to make these family calls. So he'd been sniffing around to find me because nobody else wanted to. Smyth spoke like a man of three persons: sad, sorry and succinct. Knowing these wiry sorts of business-men, he was someone who, in a month's time, would be picking up the fee for a foreign call and negotiating a price for the unnecessarily exorbitant fare. Solicitors liked to deliberate on everything, it is part of their nature. You'd think the attribute was given at birth. 'Nurse make this one a man of law!'

'You know,' I said too cheerfully, 'I'd been thinking about coming back, you've given me the perfect excuse. If it hadn't been true, I'd have said it anyway.' That last statement wasn't quite correct, I wasn't that creative.

'Ah,' he said, not following, just assuming to articulate his piece. 'It was a peaceful end, I hear from The Home she'd been in, that is. Anyway, my reason for calling is... is to tell you she leaves you soul heir to a small cottage in London, North-west. We need you to sign some papers. Sorry for your loss.'

They sounded like a standard set of words with a few changes to the paperwork. He was used to delivering them to bemused relatives. Part of a stockpile of vocabulary and vernacular they must learn in classes. 'How to deliver sad news and see the potential for your company in managing the affairs.' I admit I was not expecting this extra piece of news, but in the profession I had just left, end-of-year bonuses had become standard issue.

'Oh I see,' I said, checking my watch. There was a late flight on Friday and this man had just given me the reason and the stimulus to set fair for home. I would not only make it, I *had* to make it. It was not what I was expecting but it was a ticket out of this place with the prospect of a financial benefit.

'Thank you for calling me. I'll travel home immediately. I can meet you at her flat, this Monday, if you'll give me the address. We can proceed from there: forms, agreements, signings.' I said, anticipating the next wave of practicalities. I hung up before he did and within five minutes there was a text stating the address.

At last a genuine reason to get back to London. A city where no one cared for anyone particularly, and particularly exciting things happened. Poor Aunt Annie; she'd been in a nursing home for nigh on a year. Her cottage will be a preserved mess. Funny how a distant, dead aunt would be the one to make me reconnect with the urban world again.

I paid the final bill on my room at L'Auberge; a bed, a meal and many midnight shots. I'd enjoyed them at first and then I enjoyed the numbness they'd bring to soulless, monotonous nights. I'd try and steal away to the back of the bar and hide from

Mrs Delia Luthwaite's animated discussions on the build-up of mouth-ulcers due to hidden sugar levels in alcohol. She would have to find someone else to bother. I was leaving, I was gone. In a few days the sight of my face would be an impression and then a blur and then washed out altogether and replaced by another gullible fool.

·································

The cottage was on Latimer street. I made no claim to it by calling it *my* cottage. Attachment and ownership were not words to credit my name. It was, after all, my aunt's home, she had lived the same thirty years under its roof as I had on this planet. I would place the sale with an agent and these would be my first and my last steps down Latimer street.

I left the uncrowded tube station, Latimer Street. It felt as if they'd given up modernising this end of the rail: lights flickered on and off and tape covered broken ticket machines. With an air of irritation, I began walking down, what my American colleagues would have called, a boulevard: a long, wide, straight and changeable street. Infrequently, large cars on either side zoomed up and down the road, leaving a heavy echo to run through the pavement and into my tread or to bounce off the double glazing like the eroding wake of the sea. The cars never seemed to stop and park but drove ferociously from one end to the other in search of an exit.

The mixed architecture of Latimer street was a living example of the history of Britain. Neither sides of the street seemed to match one another so I focused on the side I walked, northwards. It was dominated primarily by a section of Victorian terraced houses. The small front rooms were sadly unkempt: the paint was cracked, the wallpaper peeled or walls lay bare, the torn curtains were held by loose thread. The little muddy gardens were a miscellaneous mess, some had been tarmacked as carports, others were a home to upturned wheelie bins, dumped sofas or children's toys and tricycles; a washing line was entangled around a privet hedge.

War damage had given way to a seventies new-build section of utilitarian flats, ugly but functional, housing ten times as many people as a whole, humble parade of Victorian homes. It was a mystery as to what my aunt's cottage might behold; I held no reservations, I could not be excited or disappointed. It was an object of money and that was all.

If my watch was slow, I'd be on time, therefore I could not consider myself late. Further up ahead of me I spotted a short, balding man with a file under his arm and a set of keys he nervously jangled. He was the only human around. Two scruffy, fat dogs had just been let out to urinate against their garden wall.

When a car passed, Mr Smyth (I had remembered his name and rolled it over in my mind) seemed to sway at his fixed spot from the energy of its speed. This was, without doubt, the man to meet me. Immediately I could see his discomfort in the strange stillness and then the sudden thundering of a single car, one at a time; it was hard to believe anyone actually inhabited this run-down street. We shook hands, made our introductions and went inside. He had taken the liberty of making enquiries as to the valuation of the house and, if I was interested in selling, he would, well, as he put it: 'deal with the whole affair.'

How sensible I had thought. This matter will be out of my hands and the money in the bank before the end of the year. It was October. Why did I feel there was an urgency? I guess people always think there is, so I played with the same notion, however false it felt, it seemed the right one to go with.

Number 85, 'Cherry Tree Cottage' read a mouldy round template. There was a dead, overly large tree in the tiny entrance garden; some seasons ago it must have been cherry. The cottage, as labelled, was not what it really resembled in a dictionary's delightful description of 'a cottage.' It was on the corner of a short side-road that housed a commercial skip and communal rubbish bins for another set of homes nearby. In location, the cottage was about two thirds of the way up Latimer Street before you met a busy junction. The traffic at this cross-section was rowdy and congested. There was an illuminated supermarket on one corner and on the other a queue had formed for the greasy-spoon, fried chips and pie shop.

The cottage was two small rooms deep on the ground floor: a basic kitchen and sitting room. It was not as untidy as it could have been, a neat, practical layout, I thought. The narrow hallway, filled with a year's worth of junk mail, had a steep staircase up to a landing with one simple bathroom and one large bedroom. The whole place was cold and damp and slightly musty. Smyth made some notes while I satisfied my curiosity, staring out at a grassy back-garden of overgrown buddleia bushes and dead hanging baskets. It was a sorry, run-down, ugly sight. I had to stay positive and would rely on an agent's charm to sell its qualities. It was capable of being a sweet, homely comfortable cottage, however peculiar the area. And yet it would not be me investing in a warm snug future for the place. I had the feeling it hid all sorts of potential problems: rising damp, crumbling brick, rotting timber-frames, squeaking floorboards beneath curling carpet, not least the money required to make it healthy and liveable again.

I stumbled to the front window of the bedroom and sat mournfully at my aunt's desk. She had always been good with birthdays and Christmas, I remember she was one of the select few who still liked to write things down: addresses, shopping lists, messages, must-do notes. She had no need or understanding of modern technology, she did not even have a television. She was, and had stayed, as she'd always been, an observer, an onlooker of life. Quite what she would have seen from this quiet, offbeat spot to draw any interest was a mystery, but this was a harsh thought and not a true inspection of her outlook. I stretched out on the unsteady chair, it did not like my form, and pulled over a black book, landscape in shape, the only item on the table. I opened it. It was lined and fairly heavy, the pages were made of thick cotton paper. She had very neat, slanted handwriting; a fountain pen with navy blue ink I guessed, and then by odd chance I felt my foot roll over that matching pen on the floor. I popped the dried-up item in my pocket; there was not a squidge of ink inside. It appeared she kept some kind of logbook, entitled 'The Circus comes South' at 'The Ground-work Theatre.' It was dated 18 months ago. Six months later she'd been taken in to a home.

Staring blankly out of the window, I watched a dull, grey London morning descend. An unscheduled, wind-swept rain began to fall upon the sill adding to the damp; a cold covering of abandonment oozed out of every bland wall. My vision is often marred by my feelings, and in most cases I have set the scene and mood of a place before looking around more generously at any positive kind of aspect. So it came as a surprise to look across from my aunt's window and see a relatively small, local theatre, 'The Ground-work Theatre,' spread on one level with a boarded-up double-door entrance and a small back door. Underneath the once luminescent, theatrical exclamation of its name, hung a bold red banner: 'Under-offer,' it declared. Sometime back, how far back seemed impossible to calculate, the sun had set on this theatre and its glamour gone with the last beam. The once distinguished place with its gayness and fun, its painted make-up and its cheers and squeals of delight was now aged, the youth and the money sucked from its soul. No longer the centre of attention and excitement, the lights of its life had been extinguished. Just outside stood a street lamppost, still alight despite the day, a spotlight to emphasise the sadness. How pathetic and deserted the theatre looked. Kicked and bruised and forgotten, the days of its life reduced to a weak heap of bleakness.

I turned back to the logbook my aunt had compiled with more interest and started to read her simple hand. It appears she kept an account of the cast and characters of the last show it performed, 'The Circus comes South.' There was a main cast of six names, then a small band of three; two café staff, one 'box-office' and one caretaker. She must have taken their names from the local paper or a flyer for the show. How she had worked out who was who was simply a matter of her intrigue and her patient mind. The cast and caretaker entered the theatre via the back door and those others via the front. She had dated their entry and exit times, their appearance and a few distinguishing features. There were two matinees a week and six evening performances. Once you had flicked through the pages and slipped into her mindset, it was not entirely cryptic; it made perfect sense. For an elderly lady with much time, little occupation and clearly in need of stimulation and companionship she must have felt quite elevated; a window box of her own making onto a theatre she could not venture to. When the curtain came down for the last show, which had only run for four weeks and which my aunt had not missed a single record, the curtain came down for the whole theatre. It closed on the last night. The End, she had written, and smudged the final two words on closing up her book.

I closed the logbook and gazed out of the smeary window once more, this time I leaned across the desk and looked harder as if the picture before me might change, and then oddly it did. Someone had stopped at the theatre. An old gentleman with a stick unlocked the backdoor methodically and I watched him scuttle inside. He was tall and thin and dressed in a long brown coat and a hat. I turned immediately to my aunt's book and looked for a Monday, today was a Monday. The date, a Monday, the Backdoor, entry time 11.30am, caretaker Leo Jones, brown coat, hat and umbrella, exit time 12:30. Her eyes were better than mine, it must have been an umbrella not a stick. Fair enough. I did not doubt her, not this time. I fanned the contents of the book, he seemed the most frequent of visitors. Appearing for an hour each morning and evening with the exception of Sunday on which no record was logged, for no performances took place. It was all perfectly logical. Dear old man, can't stop returning to the place he worked, I thought. They get into routines they can't break; habits and rituals, probably doesn't even know the theatre's for sale. Unless the agents keep him on to maintain the place before it finally does sell. Probably be bulldozed for more high-rise flats. My thoughts trailed back to myself and quite selfishly considered my own situation: best to get this cottage on the market before the planners start their hammering and digging and these little bricks shake and the windows are dislodged and a quaking vibration sends the foundations askew. The new will overshadow the old, just as logical thought outweighs an irrational one.

After a short, brisk business conversation with Mr Smyth, we said our farewells. He speedily left Latimer street like a man being stalked by his shadow. He was gone, and the street stayed empty of traffic. There was the very distant sound of school children in a playground; a plain van was making a drinks delivery to the mini-supermarket. In the very far distance, a sight I had paid no attention to before, was a vast stadium. No, not a stadium, I squinted again, a prison: Scrubs Prison. I shivered, crossed the road, not bothering to look, and went to the back-door entrance of the theatre. I tapped and slipped myself in through the slight opening. The dust was palpable.

'Hello?' I coughed the question, and again, 'Hello, do you mind if…?'

An answer came, 'Hullo, it's you… come through… watch your foot there.' The old caretaker made small steps to meet me. He did have a dark-grey moustache, I'd seen it in my aunt's logbook, after the second week she'd stated her observation. What keen eyes she had.

He beckoned me to follow him and I did with caution and with great curiosity.

'I'll give you's a brief tour... then I'll show you's where we keep them brooms. Name's Leo.' He said.

'I'm Henry.'

'You's look too young.' He said.

I proceeded to follow the gentleman, he seemed very attached to the theatre, sweeping dust and ticket stubs into corners filled with more dust and ticket stubs with an added accumulation of nut shells and plastic cups. As we approached points of interest, he would shout out their name like a foreign language lesson for beginners, 'Stage; Dressing room, one for males, one for females, two to clean; back corridor; front corridor; then bar and sitting area. I go 'round in circles, twice a day 'cept Sunday, day of rest!'

The stage was in the round with two-tiered seating in four sections, with room for approximately eighty to hundred people. On the stage sat a couple of old leather-backed chairs, a foot-rest and a stool. There was a low, round table with a cut-glass decanter and two glasses. There were four bales of hay and a pair of jester shoes and four sets of two steps for the actors to enter and leave the stage from different angles. Looks like it would have been quite a good show, I thought. We passed by a moveable rail of colourful, circus sequined costumes and country-and-western-style clothes.

Leo, the caretaker, said very little; it was awkward for him to speak, he became breathless very quickly and shuffled his feet as if they ached him. I found there were no questions I could ask him, everything was self-explanatory. He led me to the bar area, which was at the front of the theatre. The walls were adorned with posters from previous shows, 'A Beast of Burden,' 'Flowers in the Attic,' 'Fantastic Friends and other People's Company.' There were over twenty different performances, all with a small ensemble. Through one of the dirty, stained theatre windows I saw my aunt's cottage and my eyes darted to her upstairs window, her observation platform. It was far easier and clearer to view scenes from her window than it was to see out of theatre and when the front bar was lit it must have looked so light and bright, it simply invited an interest.

'Now you's seen yourself round we'll go to backroom,' said Leo, I liked the bluntness of the man. Then he mumbled, 'come for me job... knew one day they would... out to grass, that's me.'

'Er, very well.' I said, smiling at his humour and wishing to oblige him. Leo did not look at me once. He was a silhouette of odd quirks. I looked at my watch, it was 12:10. Twenty minutes and he'll want to leave. These old types keep their timings well and being part of the theatre crowd, timing is everything. My aunt would have noted this. Her sharp eyes were her best sense.

The backroom took us to just beside the stage-door exit, the door through which we had both entered.

''ere's the brooms, mop, bin and bucket. This'll be your area when you start. Now put your name and number on the blackboard and we'll be gone.'

There was a small blackboard in the broom-room and there in scratched white chalk were all the names I had seen written in my aunt's logbook: six cast, three band members, two café attendants, one box office, and one caretaker: Leo Jones. The difference was, that after each name was a contact phone number. Leo nodded his head where a slim piece of chalk rested on the edge of a dusty ledge and, feeling prompted and pressed I added my name to the list. Henry Simmons 07895 697698. Apart from Leo's phone number, the rest of the crew's numbers were rubbed or smudged, certainly indecipherable. Not one would be possible to contact, not now, not after 18 months.

Dear old man thinks I'm applying for a job, to join their theatre, he really doesn't know the outcome of the place. What a strange street this Latimer street is. Leo ushered me out of the door and locked it tightly behind him. I wanted to shake his hand but he waved me off, he turned and very slowly tottered off down Latimer street.

'Thanks then… Leo,' I cried, but the roar of a single car drowned the sound of three simple words. Only I had could have heard them.

At 12.31 I was making my way down the other side of Latimer street, away from its jagged paving and uneven surfaces, and the folk that were there or not quite there, one couldn't tell which.

....

The following year, Easter arrived late. By the end of April my aunt's cottage was sold, the sale price had dropped three times over and yet it warmed me to know the money was sitting in the bank, rising favourably from an increase in the current bank rate.

Still without obligation or purpose and keen to sample another culture, I decided to take myself off once again; this time to the Italian Riviera. It even sounded better, more mellow, more flowing, more acceptably loose and less nosy. On the start of my second month in Amalfi we were pushing in to an extremely hot June with little sign of the heat abating when my phone sang its fanciful tune. This time I found it intrusive. Nonetheless, I could not resist its stressy-desire to hold my ear. Some habits never die, I thought.

'Henry Siddons?' asked the American caller on an English number.

'Yes, who's this?'

'Hi there, name's Ralph Thornhill. I've just purchased The Ground-works Theatre... the theatre on Latimer Street in Londinium.'

'The Ground-works?' The name unexpectedly stabbed me in the foot, as if a coconut had fallen on my toes from a great height, but I was too fascinated to yell ouch. I just listened to the man and why did the irritating American use the Latin name for London? Trying to be amusing and clever in one word, perhaps.

'Yeh... The Ground-works. We took your name and cell-number from the broom-cupboard, from a blackboard inside that room. Well you see, me and my team... that is we, we want to turn the place into a museum of theatre and we're looking for anyone who can shed a light on its past.' He paused for a Hollywood-style effect, 'I went to one of those shows a few years ago... swell it was... I kinda liked the place... thought I'd give a bit back, you know. It's run itself through a rough patch and all.'

'Me, why should I know anything?' I answered curtly, 'you'd better ask Leo Jones, he's the caretaker there… I imagine, he'll know a thing or two.' I was glad to blurt out another name and get the man out of my ear and chewing on someone else. It was like trying to rid your poor shoe of stuck gum.

'Oh! Mr Henry sir, he ain't around no more. He died with the last show, 'The Circus and something.'

'The Circus comes South, you mean.' How undeniably quickly it rolled off my tongue.

'Yep that's the one alright!'

Why are the Americans always so cheerful? Is it their candy? Every little thing so sugary-sweet sincere.

'Dead? But that's impossible… you see I saw… I mean, I went…'

'You put your name on that board sir, yours is the only number we can reach.'

'So can you come on down to the theatre on Latimer street?'

The end, my aunt had written: The … End.

I hung up the phone, turned it off, picked up my feet and staggered to the indoor bar.

Henry Siddons, you were always too quick to judge people and places. You thought you could explain everything; your everything was perfectly logical, perfectly rational, just as one might assume life should be, but what about the day you walked into that theatre graveyard on Latimer Street?

THE END